D1707581

Memoirs from a Madhouse

Studies in Austrian Literature, Culture, and Thought

Translation Series

General Editors:

Jorun B. Johns
Richard H. Lawson

Christine Lavant

Memoirs from a Madhouse

Preface and Afterword
by Ursula Schneider and Annette Steinsiek

Translated by
Renate Latimer

ARIADNE PRESS
Riverside, California

Ariadne Press would like to express its appreciation to the Bundeskanzleramt -
Sektion Kunst, Vienna for assistance in publishing this book.

.KUNST

Translated from the German
Aufzeichnungen aus einem Irrenhaus
© 2001, Otto Müller Verlag, Salzburg, Wien

Library of Congress Cataloging-in-Publication Data

Lavant, Christine, 1915-1973
    [Aufzeichnungen aus einem Irrenhaus. English]
    Memoirs from a madhouse /Christine Lavant ; preface and afterword by
Ursula Schneider and Annette Steinsiek ; translated by Renate Latimer.
        p.   cm. -- (Studies in Austrian literature, culture, and thought.
Translation series)
    ISBN 1-57241-122-8
    I. Latimer, Renate. II Title. III. Series

    PT2615.A215A9413 2004
    833'.914--dc22

                                                        2004046252

Cover Design
Art Director: George McGinnis
Photo: Courtesy Otto Müller Verlag, Salzburg, Wien

Preface

By Ursula Schneider and Annette Steinsiek

Christine Lavant: A Biographical Sketch

"I became a farmer's wife in the mountains, and you?
don't tell me you're a writer?"– a girlfriend is inquiring in
a letter from 1944. Years before, in the early 1930s, the
two had met in an "Agricultural Housekeeping School."
Christine Thonhauser had been sixteen, her girlfriend a
little older, and no doubt they had discussed their plans for
the future. The village offered other careers: poultry
farming, nursery schools, horticulture, bookkeeping – such
careers were supposed to turn the girls into capable
farmers' wives or domestic servants with secure positions.
The far-reaching uncertainties of the war years – it was
1944 – made an artistic preoccupation even less
conceivable. The question implies incredulity, but even
that it is asked shows that it wasn't impossible for

Christine Thonhauser to achieve the status of a writer. It must have been a resolutely expressed desire on the part of the sixteen-year old. In 1934 she had mentioned to her girlfriend that a poem of hers had been published in a newspaper. After that they had no more contact.

Christine Lavant, born as Christine Thonhauser on July 4, 1915, was the ninth and youngest child (two of her siblings had died in infancy) of a miner and a seamstress in St. Stefan in the Lavant Valley in Carinthia, Austria. In St. Stefan brown coal was mined, and her father was a mason in the mine. The social structure of the village must have been an odd mixture of peasants and proletariat. It was an "industrial area" as she later, in 1957, described the region to a correspondent in Israel. Christine Lavant was born during the First World War, in a time of scarcity and poverty. She writes that "she was ill from the very first day of her life," suffered from "scrofula," a tubercular skin disease, which tormented her during her entire childhood and left various disfigurations on her body. Pneumonia, bronchitis, neuritis also plagued her. In addition to the physical ailments there were depression and insomnia. She tried to control her sleeping and waking states with medication.

Only if one is acquainted with the surroundings, with the circumstantial conditions of a life, is one able to assess things. The reception of Christine Lavant and her writing has excessively emphasized poverty and illness, primarily because these categories fit the cultural-historical constructs of creativity. One of these stresses the figure of the mystic and deems it more plausible that a higher power is inspiring her rather than that she can create such works of art under such conditions. Another view relies on the image of the artist as an outsider, a suffering being, and poverty and illness serve as a guarantee for this position.

Christine Lavant's letters enable us to comprehend her outer circumstances and the individual reactions more subtly. They give us an impression of the stimuli she received and how she dealt with them. "Our family malady – a reading mania – rescued me from excessive bitterness and led me into the world of alien destinies. Of course we read neither the classics nor first-rate literature but mostly just trash, the simple and sweet bread of the poor. Now and then I strayed into something more serious and so when I was seventeen Knut Hamsun's *Last Joy* struck me like a sword in the middle of my heart. Now I discovered that even the simplest and poorest life can partake of the magnificence of a destiny and I began to describe mine," she writes in her first self-portrayal, for a radio broadcast in 1950. Christine Lavant, as a child confined for long periods to bed or to home due to her illnesses, invented stories, observed instead of played with other children. In her large family, in the living room, many stories were told: people came to visit her mother for advice and comfort for various problems, and her sisters made up many a funny or spooky tale. She was surrounded by many kinds of destinies and opinions, and she learned how to

transform these into stories. The isolated Lavant Valley
was like a laboratory; not until 1936 did a pass connect it
with Styria to the north. Now there is a highway crossing
the valley, and we cannot even imagine the earlier isola-
tion. This perception freed her from confinement.

"The Lavant Valley was, until a relatively short time
ago, a basin totally sealed off from the world, which led to
many marriages within families and therefore to
inbreeding. These very peculiar destinies remind me very
much of Nordic sagas. In any case the Lavant Valley
produced until recently the greatest percentage of madmen, idiots, and suicides. My childhood consisted of many
insights into such abysmal destinies, often tinged with
humor," Christine Lavant writes in 1957 to an Austrian
cultural mediator in Denmark.

She made her first writing attempts, according to an
interview, at the age of twelve (a "novel about the transmigration of souls"); at twenty an autobiographical novel
as well as problems dealing with life and writing. During
the Nazi era she remained silent. In 1945 a butterfly
emerges from the pupa. In a December letter she writes to
the family who helped her find a publisher: "I was
sentenced to almost ten years of total inner silence . . .
Now that I have finally found a place again where I can
send my work, I am bursting forth like a tidal wave. If I
could I would do nothing but write and write only to you.
And with virtually clenched teeth I have to force myself to
do other necessary things too . . . I hope you will accept it

good-naturedly without becoming tired of me?! Because now that it has burst forth it would certainly lead to a serious inner catastrophe if I suddenly had to be silent again."

In the spring of 1946 she met her publisher Viktor Kubczak personally for the first time at the home of the writer Paula Grogger. Her guestbook reveals the pseudonym "Christine Lavant"; her publisher and her experienced colleague must have discussed and chosen the name. Perhaps her married name "Habernig" (in 1939 she had married the painter Josef Benedikt Habernig, thirty-six years her senior) sounded too regional to her publisher. Perhaps her publisher wanted to support and secure his new, unknown author with an interesting and euphonious name so that no one could lure her away. The artist herself might have feared compromising herself or others (her dead parents, her husband). With a new name she could write freely (even if she were soon recognized).

The name is well chosen: it incorporates her homeland and sounds artistic. Interestingly, the Carinthians are more likely to stress the second syllable in the name – perhaps to emphasize the name's more noble and artistic aspect. The Lavant Valley and Lavant River, however, are pronounced, like all two-syllable words in German, with the emphasis on the first syllable. Beyond Carinthia the majority pronounces her name that way too.

Immediately after the war the publishing business was not so easy. Christine Lavant's publisher had to flee from the devastated city of Breslau (Poland today), and as a German he was expelled from Austria. He had to reorganize his publishing company and apply for a license; Stuttgart became his place of publication. For every single book he had to petition the American occupation authorities for paper and printing rights. In any case there was no money. And once the books did appear there were transportation problems because of the national borders and zones of occupation between Germany as the place of publication and Austria as the most likely market. In short, the career and the business did not evolve as everyone had hoped. In 1948 the first short story to appear was "Das Kind," [The Child] in 1949 the story "Das Krüglein" [The Little Jug] and the poetry volume entitled *Die unvollendete Liebe* [Unfulfilled Love]. But most of the projected and already advertised books of Christine Lavant failed to appear after all. The publisher, for the sake of the German market, had intervened in the language of the stories and thus removed specific details characterizing persons and perspectives, which, however, were not noticed until recently when the original manuscripts were compared with the printed proofs.

When the books came out, however, they aroused interest: in August 1950 a first full-page portrait appeared in the *Klagenfurter Zeitung*, and in the same year Lavant was invited to an ambitious poetry symposium. There she met the painter Werner Berg with whom she had an intensive as well as exhausting relationship for four years.

Werner Berg's portraits of Christine Lavant – oil paintings and woodcuts – captured her image until today. Her poems appeared in magazines and anthologies. In 1952 Leykam Publishing Company in Graz printed the long story "Baruscha," her least successful work yet her favorite piece of prose. She was noticed on the cultural landscape; eyewitnesses describe her as a striking and uncommon figure. In 1954 she received the renowned Georg Trakl prize for lyric poetry together with Christine Busta, Michael Guttenbrunner, and Wilhelm Szabo. In 1956 the first of her three "classic" poetry volumes, *Die Bettlerschale* [The Beggar's Bowl], appeared in the Otto Müller publishing house, which was considered progressive with its series "Neue Lyrik" in Austria. (*Spindel im Mond* [Spindle in the Moon] appeared in 1959 and *Der Pfauenschrei* [Cry of the Peacock] in 1962.) In 1964 she received the Trakl prize for the second time: she is the only person so far to have received it twice. Ludwig von Ficker, the former editor of the journal *Der Brenner* and "discoverer" of Georg Trakl, awarded her the prize. His laudation was to be decisive in Lavant's reception. In 1968 Otto Müller, in order to maintain a public interest in Lavant, reprinted a volume of short stories: *Nell*. These were not new, which went unmentioned, and without special effort had virtually no chance with readers. And so the attempt to call attention once again to the poet's prose led directly to a long-lasting underestimation of it. In 1970 she received the great Austrian State Prize for literature.

With her letters she created a parallel writing culture. These were addressed to people in Denmark, Germany, England, Iceland, Israel, Switzerland, and Turkey, and with them she put St. Stefan on the map. Christine Lavant left few biographical documents behind: there are no diaries, no calendars, no notes – the letters represent the most important sources. They must be collected and arranged like a puzzle. In the approximately 1,200 letters gathered so far we find statements and thoughts dealing with writing and problems with writing, with ways of acting and enduring as central personal categories; we discover decisions and despair, we are able to understand influences and stimuli; we obtain information about her life and work . . .

She read like mad. In the 1950s it was primarily the "America van" that satisfied her reading mania. Lavant enjoyed this form of reeducation that presumably reached those who had been yearning for years for openness and modernity. The blue bus, a library on wheels, originating from the America House in Klagenfurt headed into the countryside once a month and offered, free of charge, modern American literature in translation: "some of it is magnificent, Truman Capote's *Other Voices, Other Rooms* and *The Grass Harp* and then William Gojem's [sic: Goyen] *House of Breath*, his first book, and in spite of the influence of Thomas Wolffe [sic] and James Jois [sic]– how the devil do you spell that? No idea, in spite of these influences, beautiful. And then, best of all, William

Sajoran [sic], Armenian, everything invigorating lovely Balkan lovely powerful colorful just glorious." The authors' names occasionally came to grief in the hundreds of pages . . . Christine Lavant spent the nights during which she could not sleep knitting and reading – "Only big American novels are appropriate for knitting" – and since she had many sleepless nights the "entire bus" was soon "read to the end." In her youth already she had read anthroposophist, Buddhist, esoteric literature, inspired no doubt by her brothers-in-law who were absorbed in these matters. Her personal needs determined the selection – her eclecticism was free of prejudice. Later on we find Jakob Böhme beside popular occultists, Isaak Lurija (Luria) beside Gurdjeff, *The Tibetan Book of the Dead* beside Martin Buber and Hildegard von Bingen. Her occasional judgment of works read remains personal. Whenever she mentions books, she is not interested in a literary critical appraisal but simply wants to inform her partner what appeals to her. If she does critique a work, it required knowledge of her aesthetic and ethical cosmos to be able to comprehend it. In a 1958 letter to the literary critic H. G. Adler, who presumably failed to grasp certain nuances, she wrote about Ezra Pound's *Litany*: "I will never be able to do that. It is so intensely solemn. My writing is like a mill wheel a barrel organ a negro drum." Other statements suggest that her "being able" refers to the inner core of poetic creation, not to the craft itself; that the notion of vital originality ("invigorating Balkan [i.e., anarchic, wild, chaotic] powerful colorful") and of an inner spiritual and perhaps also ritual connection with the work was important; and that she herself was not interested in the idea of an aesthetic creation, of a marble artifact. She felt sympathy for the direct expression; the "intensely-solemn" [quasi-religious?] was too impersonal for her, too much part of a social tradition.

She lent and borrowed books. Not just because of lack of money but because of the conviction that "not only people but also things should be where they can best be utilized" (to Martin Buber, Sept. 8, 1956). Ownership meant nothing to her: she gave and received. Friends, amused, recall situations in which she wanted to take along immediately all the books they had just finished reading to pass them on, presumably, to others. She wanted to possess only a few books. "You seem so shocked that I don't have a desk! You dear boy! Where would I put a desk? I would have to give it away at once. My library consists of two little footstools on which I stack my books, and if you touch them everything falls down," she writes to an epistolary friend in Iceland in 1958. Her stories, poems, letters came into being on the only table in her tiny one-room apartment she shared with her husband – a circumstance that no doubt influenced her opportunities to write. The situation must also have been unpleasant for her husband: the nonsmoker lived with a person who lit cigarette after cigarette, even at night.

Until the late 1950s, knitting (by hand) was an activity

she undertook to support herself. Later on her main source of income was the prizes and grants she received for her writing. She never had much money. A new stove replacing the hazardous old one, a new oil heater, a new thick blanket are so special that we can even date her letters accordingly. For Christmas 1963 she gave herself a record player, hoping for records from an admirer: "But please nothing *cheerful*! Bach, Orient, Negro, – a nice mixture, isn't it?" She often passed money along to friends and family members who, she assumed, "needed" it more urgently. "I must stop now, still have to wash the dishes and then go into town to visit a sick woman who has no one and who is also depressed often. And then I also have to visit my sister's house where misery is always at home. So you can see that now and then I have an opportunity to make use of my maternal instinct," she writes to an older girlfriend in 1956.

She didn't have any children; she exercised her motherhood in the aesthetic realm, which she confronted skeptically her entire life; she didn't know whether it was serving life or avoiding it. She was afraid of interrupting the essence of life, of not proving herself worthy of life. The often quoted sentence (to G. Deesen in 1962) "Art like mine is merely mutilated life" expresses the most painful sentiment; however, it is also not the only self-revelation of her activity. Art, and thus her writing, was supposed to serve life, and sometimes it surely served to preserve her own life, which was marked by external

12

difficulties and difficult internal phases. In a forceful and pithy manner she once expressed her view about people from the literary scene: "The most wonderful poem is not as valuable as the most ridiculous human being" (to Thomas Bernhard in July 1955). She never denied her origin and family; her sisters always played an important part in her social life. She needed and wanted her writing, but she also managed to keep it under control.

The experience of the loss of the inner possibility of writing was extremely painful for Christine Lavant. She writes that she no longer was able to find her way into the "state" necessary for creating, an inner disposition, which she associates with concepts like "mercy" or "demon." "Yes, I definitely find myself in the most distant spot from the place where I once used to write. In case there is such a thing as a rhythm I should be able to approach art again – but God knows? . . . Nothing has changed, after all, in the state of being when one of the many channels of creativity is plugged up; new ones are always emerging. Perhaps whatever it was that allowed me to write will now simply become a Negro song or an Eskimo song? Or perhaps it will pass on to you?" (to Hilde Domin, 1960)

Here she expresses an integrated notion of the creative process which also exonerates her – but the fact that she received her inspiration "from above" has nothing to do with it. There are references to her hoping that external stimuli could evoke the "state" again, as for example her trip to Turkey in 1958 when the Austrian Cultural Institute invited her to Istanbul.

After the death of her husband in 1964 and a year-long stay in the hospital, Christine Lavant left her village in 1966 and moved to Klagenfurt, the provincial capital. Her sisters and friends had enabled her to move because they expected her to feel better physically and psychically in a modern apartment with a bath and central heating (away from the old inner and outer misery). They were also hoping for new stimuli for her. But the change in scenery did not achieve the hoped-for success. Her loneliness in the highrise building, the city's first, was even greater than before. In 1969 she gave up her apartment ("reason: homesickness") and moved back to St. Stefan. Christine Lavant, hard of hearing and with poor eyesight, felt safest there, and she was fond of the *föhn*, the thunderstorms, the smells, colors, shapes. Again and again hospital stays of longer duration became necessary. And yet: there is a rough sketch of a poem (written with a shaky hand and hard to read) on the backside of the calendar pages of the year 1972.

Any one of her poems adds zest to an anthology, and in fact no one will be able to pass over it. She is the author of the most exciting poetry. Her prose is just as astounding. She wrote with precise observation, psychologically penetrating stories and such, which, like her lyrics, with their specific metaphors, still need to be understood. Only recently has she been discovered as a writer of prose. She left much undated and until now there

14

has been little in the way of a systematic order, of chronology – the poems, the stories circle each other like a mobile, they seem like splinters of an ancient continent, which still must be discovered. Most of Christine Lavant's writings are still waiting to be arranged and published. Thirty years after her death the research is a big construction site. In Austria an edition of the texts of the lyric poet, the prose writer, the epistolary artist is a work in progress.

Christine Lavant died of a stroke on June 5, 1973, in Wolfsberg in Carinthia. She is neither a Catholic lyric poet, nor a regional poet, not a working-class writer, nor a suffering woman, not a visionary, nor an autodidact, nor a natural genius. She is worth discovering.

Ursula A. Schneider and Annette Steinsiek, Research Institute Brenner-Archiv, Innsbruck, are editing Christine Lavant's *Kommentierter Gesamtbriefwechsel* (Complete Correspondence with Commentary), which is to appear in 2005. They are also collaborating on the *Kritische Ausgabe der Werke* (Critical Edition of the Works).

Memoirs from a Madhouse

I am in Section "Two." That's the observation ward for the "slighter cases," and one has a right to it only if one has done Section "Three" already. I haven't done "Three" yet, and most of the inmates are therefore resentful. Yesterday I heard the Queen say to Renate: "She marched in here with her eyeglasses and her briefcase, may the devil take her! What is she doing here anyway? Most likely spying, what else?!". . . Renate merely replied: "You're starting up again, is that it." But in the evening she came after all and said she needed the hairpin herself. Too bad! Not about the hairpin, that is, but about Renate, because I thought we could become friends. From the first day on I was attached to her already because she has such gentle, sad eyes and a pitiable nebulous smile which seems pained but isn't nearly as alarming as the laughter of the others. Incidentally, one gets used to the peculiar faces and the chatter incredibly quickly. "Oh, you better not have a look at this, you can't take it!" said Nusserl, when the tall skinny one – I believe her name is Baumerl – fell down. In order not to seem rude I had to act as if it really affected me, but in truth I would have preferred to observe everything very closely. And so they shoved me off into the washroom where I dutifully had a crying fit. But it wasn't on account of the person who had fallen down, although one could feel her screams even worse here, it was simply because one couldn't continue sitting on the edge of the bathtub without doing anything. I could very well have sung or whistled or beaten the institutional slippers against the damp wall, but I decided finally on crying. However, when it assumed such alarming proportions, it was quite embarrassing, but I couldn't do anything about it. Of course the nurses comforted me and wanted to find out all sorts of things. Well, this too will pass, in eight days not a single one will be concerned whether I cry or beat my head against the wall. Perhaps it will be Renate who will then come to smile at me in her nebulous way. But I believe she is afraid of the Queen. And she is the one who cannot abide me, just like Baumerl, and so the highest and most authoritative sides of both classes reject me virtually from the start.

I know I could change it all with one blow, for example I only needed to yield to my nausea just once during the meal distribution, I could hurl the tin cup against the wall, but I still care too much whether the nurses say "Sie" and "Fräulein" to me and whether the doctors distort their smile into something human when they come to visit me on their rounds. As long as they regard me only as a visiting guest and I also maintain this position for myself, the final border is not yet crossed.

Berta just danced. Strange that it didn't occur to any of the nurses or even to Nusserl to send me away this time. Evidently she dances rarely because the entire ward took part in it, even Nurse Minna stopped knitting her little baby jacket for a few moments, and her round, dark eyes laughed exceedingly kindly and almost with a look of satisfaction. What if I had actually approached Berta to shake her until she'd stopped? Most likely she would have scratched my eyes out. Perhaps she was even happy or at least a willing tool. But who was it who was within her? Who told her to raise her striped institutional gown above her naked, skinny knees and shake her faded strand of hair into her forehead in such a way that her pale eyes beneath it transformed themselves infinitely? Who imbued her with the peculiar rhythm according to which she strode back and forth on the brown tiles? And the high voice that resembled a singing saw and screamed forth so strangely from the toothless mouth so that one expected to come upon a little white animal at any moment. But it remained hidden, it merely sang at a high enraptured pitch for someone who perhaps was invisible in our midst. But if there are things that can be invisible among us then there must also be those that can live after us, and I have logically put myself in the wrong with my action. Of what use is it to break off a life when there is some kind of continuation? But, oh my Lord, perhaps I have already crossed the threshold and I'm no longer merely a guest but belong to all of these who still look at me as a stranger and full of suspicion? . . . What has happened? Nothing more than that a madwoman muttered confused chants: "A e i o u, what will I be tomorrow? At first I was earth, then stone, then a tree and a flower . . . But then a window opened, a large, wonderful window. A e i o u, it came toward me from all sides, and I was more than wafting woods . . . But they slammed it shut, the window, with their heavy black wings they slammed it shut. A e i o u, earth, stone and tree, and no one comprehends the word beneath the silent wings. . ."

Nothing else happened. Everyone is still laughing, and Nurse Minna, laughing, is expecting a child here. Why was it the Queen who intervened? I don't believe she did it merely out of sullenness or to prove her power. There was something in the old Hunchback that flickered like a knowing fear when she struck the dancer's neck with the blue stockings, which she was just working on. "Stop it, you mad devil!" she said meanly and couldn't care less that Nurse Minna was threatening her with the straitjacket. Her fear was different, her fear was perhaps related to mine. No, I'm definitely no longer just a guest here, and who knows how much longer the nurses will say "Sie" and "Fräulein" to me.

The doctors just made their rounds. The chief physician asked what I was writing but then didn't make any further inquiries because he probably thought I'd been too frightened by his question. My knees are still trembling so that I have to press them together just to be able to sit. But he wasn't the one. It was another one, a stranger, and only his white hair plunged me into the disconcerting error. When the chief physician introduced me to him and said: "This is the first patient in my practice who has come to us of her own accord. Of course the Fräulein doesn't really belong here, but a rural community can't afford a sanatorium with a rest cure and fattening diet, and so we're experimenting here with a little arsenic" ..., my appearance surely proved him a liar because the doctor, the stranger, smiled very dubiously. The head nurse too looked at me in an odd way and resembled more than ever a hopping, excitable bird. Only the chief physician acted as if he noticed nothing and nodded reassuringly in my direction. But I'm convinced he noticed it very well indeed, and if I don't succeed in letting him hold on to his illusions that I was frightened by his question, I will have to be very careful the next few days. Most likely he will call me in tomorrow already for a "little talk" in the physicians' room.

The Queen has just made critical comments about the rise of an entirely new trend in which third-class patients simply play the role of fine lady. The nurses encourage me with friendly smiles, however, and Nusserl says: "Just don't worry about anything, the chief physician said you may do whatever you like. The Dragon over there will calm down again." But the Dragon is not calming down. Her hump is becoming bigger and bigger, like the arched backs of testy cats, and when one of the stocking darners has to approach her to beg for the scissors, then she flies off the handle as if she would pounce on someone at any moment. "Hey, you, Krell, if you don't shape up soon, tough Rosel will come, I'm not putting up with this much longer!" says Nurse Minna very sharp-eyed. It's enough to drive one to despair! Maybe she will end up getting the straitjacket on my account. I will yet have to overcome my fear and disgust and beg the Hunchback for a pair of hose. Maybe then she'll lose some of her aversion toward me.

I have now endured the third completely sleepless night, and I'm so much at the end of all my strength that I don't want to resume the battle with Krell. Too bad, however, that Renate's newly awakened affection will now disappear again. She always had such a heart-wrenching way of smiling at me consolingly whenever I had to go to the Hunchback for scissors. Although she herself was afraid of her, she always wanted to go in my place, but I would thus have lost face once and for all before everyone. Odd how the whole wing always participated in our battle, even the second-class patients who formed an entirely segregated circle among themselves. Frau Baumerl had a way of squinting mockingly over her eyeglasses, so that I sometimes wished from the bottom of my heart she'd have a seizure. Evidently nothing is as infectious as hostilities. Sometimes I feel as if I consist of nothing but hatred. Whenever Krell for example looked at me with her eyes of fury and added spitefully: "Won't the Fräulein exert herself too greatly?," then I understood how the nurses can often tightly lace up a straitjacket with an expression of delight. Maybe I would have held up a few more days and finally succeeded in bending the Queen if I had been able to sleep at night. The commode is standing next to my bed. Every fifteen minutes at least someone is groping her way along the railing of my bed, glowing eyes staring at me, incomprehensible words are being murmured above me, and sometimes there's even an apology among them. I clench my teeth and place the second pillow over my face, but when the night nurse comes I have to place it again properly under my head. She can't stand me. During the first night she took a serious interest in me and it was obvious she felt sorry for me. But she wanted to know so many things. Whether I had an unhappy love? . . . "Does it always have to be that?" I countered with derisive exaggeration, and I shouldn't have done that. "So why did you want to shoot yourself?" she asked, slightly hurt, and when I said laughingly: "But my dear nurse, I only took a few pills," she rushed off totally offended. I'm sorry. She has a handsome distinct face and certainly meant well at first. But all this confounded questioning! If I knew at least whether the chief physician was behind it! Actually that's not like him, he could just as well ask me directly, however the fact that he doesn't do it, strikes me almost as suspicious. He probably thinks a woman to woman talk is easier. Well, if he knew who it is he'd surely go about it more discreetly. Don't think, just don't think about it!! Better to think of the major's wife, of Hansi, and of all, all the others who are here and suffer, suffer. No, I will not succumb to hate, I will go so far as to love Krell and

Baumerl and the night nurse and the face of Minna when she, beaming with evil, tightly laces a straitjacket. What will become of this child she is carrying if she has such a face? Women in a "blessed family way" should be forbidden to work in an asylum. What is to become of a creature continuously exposed to these radiations of hatred and misery? If only I think of the major's wife . . . hour upon hour and like clockwork, day and night, she leaps up in her bed. "Austria be damned! The czar of Russia be damned! The entire world be three times damned and cursed. They murdered my husband, my glorious, proud husband. Damn! Damn! Damn!! May the devil take everything that's still living!" Her eyes glowed like coals, her white disheveled hair stood on end like wires, and her hands were like elongated bird claws. Hour upon hour she goes on like that, and even the snoring of the singer with the full beard which fills the entire ward vanishes like a breeze before this outburst. Sometimes I am waiting for it as if for a deliverance since then one can't hear – at least not for the duration of a few minutes – Hansi's whimpering. Hansi is only twenty years old, she's been lying here for an entire year already, and three times a day, every day, she is being fed through a tube up her nose because she has evidently resolved to starve herself. She is only a mere skeleton, but at one time she must have been perfectly lovely. Her bluish-black hair usually falls from her bed down to the floor. In the afternoons when her mother comes she lifts up the hair like a sacred treasure.

Even the major's wife sometimes abruptly breaks off cursing, even before her son arrives. The nurses become helpless like sheep in the presence of this mother, and even Friedel, eternally singing, disappears every time. Hansi's husband comes every other day. He is an officer, higher up, like the son of the major's wife, and when they happen to meet by chance, both blush with sorrow or shame. Mountains of agony grow here eternally, but the summits are formed by those who come here daily with love and depart with despair. One can't look into their faces, one simply couldn't bear it. It is shameless anyway to be present, and yet the only reason I lie down at noon for a few hours is to be present in the ward during visiting hours. And here I already know everything by heart. The narrow bent back of the old lady when she lifts her daughter's hair from the floor, her husband's broad, helpless shoulders with which he always wants to conceal as much as possible the roses or carnations which he places on the bed cover and very close to his wife's face. Ah, how they always keep on expecting something from this face! The slightest sign of recognition, a smile, perhaps only the reflection of an earlier smile, or a changed tone in her whimpering. But nothing happens and changes. Softly and high-pitched and at almost calculated intervals the eternally same tone pierces the ward, again and again one thinks of a young kitten caught in thorns. How often must this mother's heart have been pierced?! No, I don't know her face and never want to know it. Her back and the pale curve of her hand which often trembles for seconds above the forehead of her whimpering daughter suffices for any statement. Sometimes before she leaves the ward, she turns momentarily toward the bed of the major's wife. Two mothers, two old society ladies, two endlessly suffering women. The air around both becomes glassy and thin, and often the son enters at this particular moment. He greets Hansi's mother almost like a saint, he greets or sees no one else. With several long steps he is at his mother's bed and kisses her hand. This hand is now no longer a bird claw, it is the most refined and most reticent imaginable. Someone always casts veils over these two, and only with closed eyes can one surmise what is really happening. It is not truthful to say that the son is always opening a newspaper and reading softly from it, nor are the few sentences they say to each other in French, nor is the rattling of the bed railing louder and more abrupt whenever they move. No, all this happens only super-ficially, outwardly, somehow like an impenetrable glass cover over something infinitely precious. Inwardly they take great delight in each other. I know it, I sense it, when I am lying in my bed with eyes closed. Changes still transpire here which are in no way inferior to a miracle. She is no longer a madwoman, raging and cursing, not the slightest trace of hate resides in the old aristocrat during these hours. As Christ walks on water, this mother walks on the sea of her madness in the presence of her son. And he believes her. Not for a second is he afraid she could suddenly fall in again. And she doesn't fall in. She never breaks through until the last door of the asylum has shut behind her son, but then it turns terrible. It is as if an entire inferno wanted to revenge itself because she had been banished for an hour from her possession. But one can no longer say it with words, it is almost more devastating than the sight of the Crucified One. I wonder if I will ever have the desire or the courage to laugh again after the weeks here? Oh, perhaps very much so? Perhaps one should even begin to learn to laugh in such places to possess it and never lose it again. Krell just walked by and said softly she would shred me into dust and ashes. I smiled at her. But I am afraid. Maybe I should try to forge ahead to the teachers' table? Everyone seems so well-behaved there, and one often wonders instinctively why they are even here in the first place. But as a third-class patient and uneducated it won't be easy to penetrate this circle of the upper ten thousand. When I merely pass by them they all look at me so dismissively, only the fat Goethe expert who sleeps in the same ward as I do permits herself a little smile sometimes. Should I ask her for "Wilhelm Meister"? Maybe she will then want to quiz me about it, and I have no intention really to read the book.

I failed, failed completely. When I appeared, two of them started at once to speak Italian. Baumerl indicated quite bluntly that patients who are here at the public expense of their committees had the moral duty to work. Her eyes were so clever and serious I wanted to ask her:

"Why is it that all of you dislike me?" But thank God the red-haired rosary-sayer had a seizure, during which Baumerl stood by her like a mother, quickly taking off her jacket and shoving it under her head. She also forced something between her teeth so that she couldn't bite through her tongue. No, I never wish a seizure on Baumerl again, no matter how scornfully and disparagingly she looks at me. I now understand everything much better on the whole and I will never sit down again at the teachers' table. How embarrassing it was for all when von Rauschbach, the little one with the dark eyes and snowy-white locks, suddenly turned to me and asked whether I had seen the flying horses too. It was in the middle of a conversation about French literature that she asked me this question and I was clumsy enough to say "yes." What a pity that one often becomes tactless in surprising situations. I should have realized I am not entitled to oblige any of them with indulgence. Had I laughed out loud and said: "Don't talk such crazy stuff!" surely no one would have held it against me. But none of the others forgave me for this gentle, shameful "yes," which transported von Rauschbach, the little one, to ecstatic laughter. I still feel exposed to all the indignant and simultaneously helpless eyes. Not one intervened verbally, they probably know from experience that ordinary words are no match for the flying horses, and they most likely did not want to resort to others in my presence . . . "We were in Naples, and the *Herr Regierungsrat* (Government Councillor) was just in the process of making me a marriage proposal, you know, under palm trees and cypresses by the blue sea, he was a man of taste and culture, he quoted the ancient wind from the sea, and I was just going to point out to him that it wasn't Capri, and besides, there was also no budding fig tree, but after all that isn't of any importance, is it, he no doubt must have meant the Waves of Sea and Love, but then these flying horses appeared and they had golden manes. Some believe they were shod with silver horseshoes that bring luck, but I don't necessarily want to insist on that. What is your opinion? I can't stop laughing when I think that a man of rank and culture can cling to flying horses with golden manes. Isn't that absolutely comical? Someday I'll publish a volume bound in nothing but golden horse hairs. That's a brilliant idea, don't you think? Listen, the next time you come to Naples . . ." I don't know what would have happened next because the Goethe expert, without any trace of a smile, took me along and led me into the dormitory where she handed me a book from under her pillow. "Go off by yourself, sit and read it alone," she said, and that was blunt enough.

Unfortunately Nurse Marianne is on day duty today and she is so obvious in displaying her antipathy towards me that Frau Lanzinger doesn't dare to invite me with a smile. At other times she did it occasionally when she noticed how much of an outcast I was. She is always embroidering a scene with a castle and palm trees, and if one admires it she becomes as trusting as a child. Her husband is living at present with another woman, and even though she is married and already has a half-grown daughter, she still has to work here. She does it with a good-natured, kind sluggishness that never lets itself get carried away to any kind of extreme measures. I believe it must be the scenery which she is embroidering with such devotion. No doubt she often inhabits for hours the castle with the terrace and has no idea what is in reality transpiring around her. Sometimes she tells me in a low voice about her young friend for whom she has only "maternal feelings." Still, now and then, she can blush so sweetly that one would like nothing better than to embrace her. Nurse Marianne is without a doubt the most intelligent and inwardly purest one here, and I'd be very happy if she could take a liking to me, but heaven knows why she doesn't. Of course I also try to counter her with antipathy, but I never quite succeed. Just now, for example, she passed by and glanced at the Crucified One and it was not a nurse's glance. It contained something inconsolable and a great deal of courage. But surprisingly Agnes let her pass without swearing at her! None of the nurses and even less so a physician manages to get past her without being observed and screamed at like an animal: "Let me die, let me die for the sake of God's mercy. For the sake of Christ's suffering, kill me!!" Her whole body writhes, and she wants to raise her hands and fold them and can't, because they have to clutch at the wall, no, claw into it, and surely she must sometimes think she would be heard if only she could fold her hands correctly, and then she overcomes her terrible dread of the fall, she removes her claws from the wall and collapses like an animal. Not until then, on the floor, when there is no longer an abyss beneath her into which she could sink, does she yield to the frenzy of folding her hands. Like wings they beat up and down, like weapons she hurls them up from below, like ropes she winds them around the feet of passers-by. During the first few days I had to let myself fall down and cradle her head on my knees, but such things are not easily forgiven here. "Don't be a fool," Nurse Minna said and then, during the breakfast distribution, she withheld my exempted coffee. But when she saw that I choked down the brown roux soup in spite of my aversion to it, she became somewhat charitable and felt she had to comfort me: "Don't believe that they have much pain. The one with breast cancer in your ward is much worse off. Of course it's unpleasant not to be able to hold oneself erect; she has an equilibrium-disturbance, you see, that's why she is always falling down when she lets go of the wall. But you mustn't worry so much about things around here, the chief physician also doesn't like to see his patients worry, after all that's why we are here, you see, and tomorrow you will get your coffee again, I simply ran out of it today." That was her way of offering comfort, and I had to smile at her as if nothing were as important to me as my breakfast coffee. In front of the Crucified One, however, on the floor, stood the tin cup with the soup, and she lapped it up like an animal. She seems to be between thirty and forty, and so she may well live another twenty years and these twenty years will be spent clutching at the wall like a crucified being or being thrown on the ground like an animal. Her words will consist of nothing but: "Kill me, for God's mercy kill me!" But no one will do it, everyone keeps clear of her in order not to be caught in her clutching, beseeching hands. Nurse Marianne looked at her inconsolably yet courageously. May she be blessed for it, even though she dislikes me a hundred times. Even though her courage is not the one Agnes so desperately seeks. No, that's not what Marianne intended. She is said to be deeply religious. So she must have meant a different courage, a higher courage, but one that won't help any other heart but her own. Or did Agnes sense help after all? Why did she lower her face, distorted with pain, before this gaze as if she had been overwhelmed? As if someone had made her a future promise? Again and again I keep thinking here that physicians should actually all be priests and nurses all nuns. Because the suffering here goes so far beyond anything human that it can't possibly be countered by something merely human.

Nusserl, for example, is good. She is also the only one who now and then detaches the Crucified One from the wall and, embracing her like a child that one teaches how to walk, guides her up and down the hall. Yet Nusserl came here from an orphanage to do this difficult work, never knew her mother, probably never has been guided lovingly herself. However, she is also expecting a child, which may inspire her with this touching, gentle warmth, so that all are compelled to love her and can't help but call her "our Nusserl." But what a difference there is between her and Minna when both are sitting at the nurses' table and working on their baby things. Each one is in a state of happiness, but one isolates it, keeps it to herself and when she looks up becomes sober and hard at once, whereas the other one remains soft no matter what she does and gently shares her happiness without lessening it. I actually never fear for the child that Nusserl is carrying. Since she shares so much love she must be living safely as if within a tower. No one . . .

I was called away to the physicians' room, where the court psychiatrist was waiting. Nurse Friedel brought me there and gave me one more comforting pat in front of the door: "Have courage, my child, he won't eat you. Just don't let him intimidate you." . . . But I wasn't fearful in the least and couldn't even imagine anything. The chief physician was there and the head nurse (I could have done very well without her excitable giddiness) and also a short, bald gentleman, a stranger, upon whom I now belatedly and sincerely wish a daughter who, after a suicide attempt, finds herself harassed by a court psychiatrist. But naturally she would be a lady, and therefore everything would be entirely different from the very beginning. "So this is the person?" was the first thing I heard from his mouth. The chief physician smiled a little obliquely, he must not have felt very comfortable with this opening. "So you wanted to take your life. Don't you want to tell us why?" The head nurse bounded to the window and from there looked at me with piercing eyes, the chief physician was still smiling at the floor, and the desk lamp was mockingly reflected in the bald pate of the short psychiatrist. I laughed. It was a stupid and no doubt repulsive laughter, and I realize it didn't contribute to making me more sympathetic to the short psychiatrist. "We don't have much time," he said meanly, and to the chief: "Is she even in a condition to be interrogated?" . . . He momentarily looked up in an odd way and said: "I believe so." . . . "All right, then!" the beast of a fellow continued to probe impatiently. I answered stubbornly: "I simply don't want to." . . . "But you have to have a reason. Most likely your boyfriend left you and there wasn't another one right away?!" . . . "There never was one at all." . . . "Well, then, why don't you now tell me how things are at home. You still have parents, what do they say when you behave like that? Well?" . . . Here the chief physician interjected the words distress and misery, which of course is exaggerated, but either this was indeed the image he received from my intimations, or he simply wanted to help me out a little. The short psychiatrist asked him: "But why is it that she's not working? Even if she appears to be somewhat frail, she still could assume a less demanding job, and work drives away all sorts of stupidities which these young ladies sometimes encounter at a certain age. From school directly to a decent, stern workplace: that's still the best remedy for hysteria. Well, maybe you'll have her under control in a year so that she can be put up somewhere." . . . "All she wants to do is write," said the sharp voice from the window. Everyone laughed, why shouldn't I have laughed too? . . . "Well, my dear – " said the short psychiatrist, "of course you will just have to break yourself of these habits. Write with a capital W, probably she can't even spell decently, but she wants to write! You see, my colleague, that's what happens when every coal miner thinks he has to send his offspring to get an education and such. So, my child, just leave writing to others, and after the chief physician has brought you back to your senses, say after one or two years, then be happy if you get a lady who trains you properly for all domestic duties. Understood?" I turned fiery red with rage, the chief physician must have thought I was red from fear, because he secretly raised six fingers under the table to indicate I needed only the six weeks here for my arsenic cure. No, I do realize that he couldn't make it easier for me; since the community has to cover the costs here, it must also have the corresponding documents and confirmation that I am indeed crazy. Well, that will be lovely when I return home again. But I had to take it into account when I applied for admission here. What was I expecting? A cure? Did I really think that such and such amount of arsenic, taken at certain intervals, would lend meaning to my life? That it could make me beautiful or only courageous and cheerful? Naturally I

didn't believe it for a moment, but where else should I
have gone after this dreadful thing that went awry. Thirty
pills, three days and four nights of death-like sleep, and
then to awake again and find everything totally unchanged
and the same as before, and the mother's mute, petrified
face, and the sisters who obviously did not believe in the
"flu." Until now Mother had never before withdrawn from
a difficult situation, but this time she was gone even before
I could get up and stand on my feet. She had left to see
Berta, in spite of her dislike for Anton. Should I still have
been there when she returned? "She will stay up there for
three days," Lui said and cried. But no one reproached me.
Father brought home medicinal herbs, he's the only one
who believes in the "flu." He'll also never find out where
I was during these six weeks, they'll probably tell him I
was in the hospital because of my ear problems. He at least
can still be looked at innocuously. Oh, good God, now I'm
already counting on simply returning home, whereas last
night I was still thinking, never again! But what else is
there, good Heavens?! A strict, decent job and no longer
being able to write and say "yes, ma'am!" and do a
thousand repulsive chores day in and day out, and for
whom and what for???? Every morning afraid of the
following day, afraid of every sort of demand that is
placed on one. To know that every object one has to touch
is full of aversion and animosity, to do every chore with
the certainty that it will be wrong. Nothing to summon up
love for, no confidence in any undertaking, because one

has never been capable of undertaking the one and only thing – to change oneself in such a way that one would be loved. Yes, they are right. At least they all come pretty close to being right when they point to unhappy love because which love is unhappier than the one which is never demanded and therefore also never attained. "You should get yourself a boyfriend," the chief physician suggested already during our first session. I replied at once soberly and casually: "Am I supposed to fling my arms around the neck of the first man to come along on the street? And just imagine if you were the one!?" Of course then we both laughed, and afterwards he never touched the topic again. It would be interesting to know of course what such people, who make suggestions of this nature, actually think of love. Do they regard it primarily as medicine, or do they believe they have to set upper and lower boundaries here too? Maybe the bald psychiatrist was right as he said upon leaving: "Another disheartening example of what happens when workers' children read novels instead of being raised to perform decent work." . . . One thing that's certain is I would not have decided to go to an asylum at my community's expense, if — no, I won't say it, I won't say it here either, and it shall remain my happiness and temptation and delight and thousandfold pain and shame and despair. Perhaps one day, before the six weeks are over, I will get into something else that's foolish, something so bizarre that the chief physician will consent to the two years or that I'll be kept here forever.

When I close my eyes and follow only the smells, I can convince myself at any time that I'm there where he is walking about and dispensing his voice and his smile, where the nurses and patients grow more silent with awe when he stands in the doorway, ah dear Lord, perhaps he passes by outside every day and now and then hears the same bird singing that I hear, smells the same grasses and trees, and the wind that's knocking against the barred windows permits him perhaps to look at the clouds . . . Why should I not be here for the rest of my life and, if need be, mend the institutional stockings day after day. One day the Queen too will accustom herself to me or I to my fear.

I will —

Anton was here and I flung my arms around his neck. In the middle of the visitors' room and in front of all the people, the strangers, the crazy patients, the two nurse supervisors. It's mainly this blasted, bald devil who is at fault, he is the one who got me down with his mocking disdain so that every face that comes from our family poverty had to strike me like heaven's mercy. Anton is good, and Beta is right in not leaving him even if he has been without work for years. He also was not ashamed of his wet eyes, and he must have dropped his otherwise so unavoidable serenity outside the door. Anton is good, and if I should ever find an Anton I could rejoice. Yes, I too would work like Beta far into the night to be able to live with such a man. He brought me books, and into one of them he placed three cigarettes and a flat little package of matches. Of course I am not going to write a satire about him. The devil take each and every one who speaks or writes a single word of mockery about someone who lives in poverty. Ah, why is it I am so indignant? Is it justified? After all, nothing happened but that a total stranger observed things around me as he could judge them from his point of view. That's the end of it!!! . . . Leschke would say: "Tempel pomadi," he happens to have his own Latin, just as he has his own vocabulary, and he gets along very well. Why did I resist starting a relationship with him? When Anton comes back I will ask him what his brother is up to. Of course a relationship is out of the question now since people like Leschke have a sense of pride too and don't choose their girls from an asylum. Beta doesn't want to come, thank God! I hope, no, I'm sure, Anton is sufficiently tactful not to describe the milieu here to her. Berta and Magdalena were with me in the visitors' room at the same time. The latter stared, as she always does, with her beautiful, contaminated, unlucky face and pretended not to see her mother at all. From time to time she looked up at Anton in a peculiar way. He immediately took an interest in her, but I couldn't tell him anything about it because I myself don't know what's the matter with her. Once when I asked Nurse Minna, who usually shares information about everything, about her, she merely said, "Oh, she's a pig, be happy if you don't know anything about it." She never talks and always pokes around in her ravaged face with her festering fingers as if she were searching for something. At night she must be getting little sleep because I often hear her bed clanking as if an animal were continuously tossing up and down. Her mother seems to be a respectable peasant woman, but maybe she is not even her real mother, because there was no sign of love or agitation in her face, nor in her hands, as she offered Magdalena an apple and white bread from her bag. And when she pushed aside her daughter's heavy golden-blond braids that hung down her back half undone as they fell on her bag as she was handing her the food items, the gesture implied something repugnant. How differently Hansi's mother touches her daughter's hair!! I will have to love Magdalena. Maybe I can force myself today already to sit beside her during dinner. Of course she won't notice it, but still! . . . Berta behaved completely differently to her visitor. It was an old man with a goatee and glasses, and if we all weren't wearing institutional gowns here, you would have to consider him unmistakenly for an inmate. He was giggling so insufferably and accompanied Berta's soft singing with such grotesque motions, and if Nurse Friedel hadn't finally intervened energetically, both would undoubtedly have started to dance together. Anton thought he was her brother, but he is only supposed to be a friend of her dead father's and a teacher in the school for the deaf and dumb. Before he left, Anton said: "You mustn't stay here one hour longer than is absolutely necessary." He also promised me to come at least every other day.

Now I'm sitting here again in my corner space, and it seems as if I had been uplifted inwardly, as after an honor that had been conferred on me. The nameless one, I call her the Ivory Countess, tends to walk now and then back and forth with quick, small steps in the hall; her long, dark skirt sweeps behind her in an enterprising yet reserved manner, and it happens very rarely that one hears her voice. Hers is a soft voice, slightly tinged with arrogance: as if she had acquired it at a steep and eternally concealed price. One is almost inclined to think she is perpetually prepared to offer her life at any time for this acquired voice and the sake of her unusual gait. And yet I don't believe that she does not esteem her life. I rather suspect that everything concerning it is very precious to her. Nurse Minna just smiled at me in passing by. Should I ask her who the Ivory Countess really is. Illusions, to be sure, are precious, but the truth is usually more important . . . Well: Her name is such and such and she was a ladies' dressmaker. I am still smiling because there is no real reason to cry. Everything here moves on totally different levels, and the directions are much more diverse than among the "normal." I feel I can preserve my Ivory Countess quite well despite the truth. I wonder if she will come to fetch me again. There are a few things I understand better now. Of course, even if some well-to-do relatives pay for her second-class stay here, as an uneducated person she still doesn't belong to the teachers' table and just as little to the others, who have to depend on public welfare. Perhaps for that reason she may have hit upon me and not, as I earlier suspected, because of certain mysterious sympathies. But how elegantly she behaved . . . "Would you be so kind as to play a game of Halma with me?" Gently, with an almost enchanting raising of her small, chiseled, silky-radiant face she had asked the question. Startled, I gave a rather clumsy reply that I would gladly play if I knew the game. Then there was a shimmer of a smile on her thin lips and she said she would teach me. And then we played . . . It did not go well, and she had difficulty hiding her impatience, but it went very nicely with her whole being. Even though I had to pull myself together as before a difficult exam, every move was in her favor. After some time she was annoyed, and it was most noticeable in her small, almost stony-looking hands, they became more and more vexed with every victory. Why did I never learn how to play Halma? Although I find the game totally insipid it might ease my stay here. I wonder whether she will ever invite me again? It would be terrible to fail before all in this matter too. The Queen must have taken a day off today and is parading her suddenly enlarged-seeming hump like a precious burden up and down the hall. The caretakers let her carry on with it, even Nurse Minna suppresses every sharp word. Maybe I often do them wrong and they are to a certain degree worn out by the goings-on here. The Skinny One, who used to lie in the second bed on my right and spend her time screaming or, after injections, sleeping like a dead person, was brought into the little room next to the toilets this morning, dying, and that's where she finally did die, alone, on the low stretcher. There were no prayers or tears, but death managed well without them. Actually I could have prayed, but my first thought was whether I could now get her bed after all so as not to spend my nights awake so close to the commode. Of course I am not entitled to a request, but it might at least occur to one of the physicians . . . So this is the famous love for your neighbor –: One dies after terrible sufferings, dies like an animal, and another is obsessed with the thought of obtaining this death-bed.

Dinner is once again behind us. I seated myself next to Magdalena, but it no longer happened out of love – how impossible this word sounds here –, it happened only to punish myself, and Magdalena was completely in the right to look through me as if through a barely perceptible object. Her tainted blood must cause her endless agony because she has scratched herself so bloody, in spite of all the warnings, that two caretakers from the men's section had to be called to force the poor woman into the straitjacket with their shameless, wild assistance. I don't know if it was in fact necessary, but surely it wouldn't have been necessary in this way, because as soon as they touched her breasts they were no longer caretakers but men, and they derived pleasure from it. Why, if there are angels, is it not incumbent on them to prevent things here on earth which should only be permitted in outermost hell.

Here I am writing this with ordinary words, writing them
matter-of-factly, and what I should be doing is demolish
the walls stone by stone to throw each one against heaven
so that heaven would remember that it too has an
obligation toward us down below. Perhaps I am cursing
myself with each of these words, but I have to write them,
it is perhaps my duty. Others have to build bridges, bring
children into this life or transpose things into sounds,
somewhere someone is perhaps painting a picture and
hates himself more with every brushstroke, ah, we all
follow the direction into which we have been cast. Stones!
Stones! Stones! . . .

I had another crying fit. Since the rounds just took
place I received my consolation so to speak firsthand and
from the source. The chief physician said: "But Fräulein,
what's the matter, what's the matter?" The assistant
physician: "My child, my child, calm yourself!" The head
nurse: "My dear, get a hold of yourself, please, you are not
alone here." . . . Nurse Minna reported: "We had to force
the Dorninger woman into the straitjacket, perhaps the
Fräulein took it too much to heart?" . . . "Well, good heavens, you have to get used to that around here," the chief
physician declared. Later on I had to go to his consulting
room again. I think his goodwill toward me has begun to
waver because his questions were backhanded and then
suddenly so abusive and right into my face like fists –:
"The night nurse reports that you have been lying entirely
awake the past four nights . . . May I ask why? . . . How, –

or . . ." It was not my mind that told me this was a moment of greatest danger for me because the mind after all is not on a level with the psychiatrist's, but suddenly I became very sharp inwardly and like the edge of a knife. My reply turned out well: ". . . Or? . . . What do you mean by or? Do you think it gives me pleasure to lie awake here? To make myself a little interesting, right, is that what you think? Yes?" . . . "Now, now, no need to get so belligerent immediately, I am not thinking anything, I am here to help, but if you lie awake night after night, it's no surprise if during the day, at the slightest provocation, or none at all, you are a bundle of nerves. You still don't know what pills you took?" . . . "No, I don't know any Latin and my memory is not particularly good." . . . "Good, I will now recommend –" . . . Here he paused for a while, probably to intimidate me with fear of his possible recommendations. He almost succeeded because I thought they might call for the caretakers from the men's section. But, should it get that far, I intended to accept the straitjacket good-naturedly. Then, as he was gently taking the blotting paper out of my hands which I had virtually shred to pieces, he continued: "I will recommend that you get a very hot bath every evening before going to bed, that will gradually calm you down." . . . Ah, and with these words he almost had me where he perhaps wants me, since the happy surprise made me so submissive I had to force myself not to seize his hands and weep. Of course he did not want me to weep on his hands, but whoever weeps like that just once is finally ready to make any statement. Or am I wrong about everything? Perhaps no thought is any longer substantiated, no conclusion correct? What if everything were so much easier, if he had simply called me to offer me a few minutes of different surroundings, to let me breathe real air, and finally to make me so happy. But no, he is not yet a clairvoyant after all, and how else would he know it – or even hit upon the idea – that a person of my circumstances can't imagine greater bliss than that of a daily bath. But, oh my Lord, what if it turns out like the first time? I was so horrified when they all took turns coming in and staring at me with their sick looks and I waited and waited and thought the nurse would surely turn them out and then leave too, but she only turned on me and said: "Hurry up, hurry up, we still have other things to do." . . . "Aren't they leaving me alone? May I close the door?" . . . But she laughed and kindly promised me that no one would bite me. The door stayed open, everyone could go in and out and stand around, and there was nothing left to do but close my eyes to pretend at least a state of aloneness. Will it be like that every evening? But after all they say "Sie" and "Fräulein" to me as they would to a paying patient, maybe they will also show me this consideration, because the paying patients are permitted to bathe with closed doors, however, under the supervision of a nurse. I wonder if one may pray for such things? It's no small matter since here it would be decided whether poor people are permitted to benefit from a good deed clearly and completely or whether for us poor dogs everything has to be distorted into a grotesquerie. I don't care! I will take a bath, every evening I will be completely clean for my own sake and at night I can envelop myself in the simple smell of my washed arms, that is more than I have ever had before. Still, I will be grateful. Gratitude is – Nurse Friedel is just waving towards me, please, God, help . . .

Ah, I'm laughing. Indeed, I'm still laughing, it's disgusting how little control one has over oneself. A laughing fit is in no way better than a crying fit, ridiculous. I'm not laughing about my shame, which was too slight, it really vanished at once when I felt the pleasure of the warm water on my body. After all it's just a matter of having something, anything, on one's body, an inter-mediate between one's own palpable being and a future self. Well, well, I am expressing myself almost like a philosopher, and just a moment ago I was lying in there like an object on display. Perhaps I should have begged? But I have to keep a promise I made to myself before I went to our mayor at home to convince him it would be cheaper and more advantageous for him to pay for my relatively short stay in an asylum rather than later on for a permanent stay. This request was a weight I could only bear if I created an inner counter-weight. And this was the resolution, that I would bear all consequences to the end. Therefore it would be shabby to want to beg for exceptions afterwards. Moreover it was Nurse Friedel who had to watch over me. This tall, slender, smart woman who is always cheerful, impudent, and almost quick-tempered – begging would have done little good with her. She was knitting a ski pullover, and while I was undressing we discussed the Norwegian pattern which she wants to knit in at the top. But at this point they appeared, entered, stood around, stared, sneeringly participated, and hid their mocking demeanor as little as they did when even Magdalena gets the straitjacket. Even though Friedel shouted several times: "Get away, leave, right now?!" – well, they left then, but others came and the same ones returned, only Renate did not come, I only saw her blurred, apathetic smile in the doorway for a vague moment, then it moved on. I used such a vast amount of soap that Nurse Friedel said because of that alone I cost the institution too much. But she laughed heartily as she said it and maintained that I looked like a boy, and then I realized I was also naked in front of her and let myself drop into the water to the tip of my nose. It was going to be lovely, without a doubt and in spite of everything. The water was rushing into my ears and kept everything else away from me, my closed eyes revealed nothing of the horrid space, and I did in fact succeed in becoming, for the time being, as isolated as I needed to be to fully obtain this beneficence. But one becomes so hideously sentimental if one is alone with oneself and wants to be restored from inner stresses, one reaches all too readily for means that are lacking in all taste. How easy and clean it would have been to think of oceans, a beach, gray with dunes interrupted here and there by a mere hint of yellow broom. But I was thinking of Nefertiti – the Egyptian Queen, yes, her of all people. Of her splendid royal face, her foreign, precious attire, of the raising of her hands when she stood somewhere at the edge of the desert and sensed much of that in her ancient blood.

It is Beta of whom I am now thinking, my beautiful, happy sister Beta, and how I used to bear her a grudge with secret estrangement when she once surprised me at home as I was softly singing to myself while doing some needlework: "I know an Egyptian fairy tale, Nefertiti; you lovely Egyptian fairy tale, Nefertiti, your splendid royal face awakens ancient dreams in me . . ." etc., etc. . . . , nothing but silly, sweet nonsense. Beta was laughing like crazy and during lunch she started out in front of all the others: "Your splendid royal face awakens ancient dreams in me . . ." Of course I joined the laughter of all the others, laughed into Mother's punishing eyes, which wanted to break Beta's tendency to ridicule, but ever since then I've remained somewhat estranged from her. And yet Beta is the one who wouldn't have to disguise herself greatly to portray a long gone delicate Queen, and Anton, this fanatic follower of Buddha, did not renounce his precious freedom in vain for her sake, although he now chides our mother, this little, gentle, and endlessly earnest mother, as a procuress, because she insisted on his either marrying Beta or giving her up. Naturally he did not give her up. For Beta is not only enchanting but also courageous and talented enough to support herself and a Buddha-follower with her work. That's how our life is. Oh Beta, you beautiful, slender, brown bird, what splendors you would taste and allow to be tasted if only you weren't the daughter of a coal miner and hadn't had to lead the life of a clever somewhat stubborn servant girl. The splendors you tasted were your mistress's cast-off clothes which you knew how to wear so that the mistress's men suddenly acquired a taste for them, and you had to give notice on the first of the following month. That is our life, marred already in all its lovely beginnings, but you don't admit it since you continue with your lovely, slender steps, sing your radio songs cheerfully and bravely, create wonderful dresses for very elegant ladies, and you yourself the prettiest of these, as if these dresses had grown from your body . . . Unfortunately nothing grows on my body except poverty, clumsily worn, humiliating for me and others. Just now in the bathroom I was thinking about being able to contain it for a long time, creating havoc with secret blood memories, thinking about being able to use them to have a place of refuge in an asylum, stared at only by mocking madmen. And then she suddenly touched me, the Queen, not the Egyptian one but the one with the hump and the innate hate. Nurse Friedel was so deeply amused that I repressed my scream so as not to destroy her mood! The Queen stood before me, her entire entourage behind her, waiting, her eyes like two very heavily laden chandeliers auspiciously turned toward my nakedness and somehow grandiose, mysterious, so that not even hate came to light anymore. As she was talking to me I had to ask myself where she suddenly had found her language. No one prompted her, at least no one visible. But she did it so expertly that her words revealed much more conviction than the laughter of the nurse, although that was surely the only sanity in the whole room.

"Today and tomorrow," she said, "and perhaps also another little half-day, then the king is within me. He comes very gently because he treads on pure water, in his hands he carries the fish that don't have enough room in the nets, and if they don't turn into gold he lets them drop like stones because he needs gold. But he will look at me as if I were a star and ask: Did you fill all of them with gold, none has been emptied and carried away? . . . Then I will simply wave to him gently, and then he will let all the fish drop, the golden ones too, and will follow me into the treasury like a star. Because I am his morning star and the salvation of all the sick. Inside I will show him all the stockings filled with pure, unalloyed gold, with which three big chests are being filled, one for him, the Lord and King, one for the holy church and one for all the poor. And then I will use one of my rays for you and will direct a beam of light at him and say: To this one with the charity-gold, give it to her, she should distribute it with mercy and justice so that she too gain worthiness with which to enter our realm. You, you, you however, must honor me for it. You, rise, and honor me!"

And so I rose, just as I was, and honored her by kissing her gnarled, dirty hand. Nurse Friedel shouted: "Stop it, children, I can't go on, oh God, I can't, my belly will burst." . . . "Let it burst, what else do you need it for?" . . . the Hunchback asked with a sneer and without any fear, but then moved on with the rest. Nurse Friedel then turned her offended self to me and asked indignantly why I was lending myself to such mischief. And I became cowardly and said: "Just because I didn't want to provoke her." . . . "Ah nonsense, we would have handled her, each one becomes docile in the straitjacket. But hurry up now, I can't just sit around with you endlessly." . . . I did hurry up then and practiced an innocuous laugh, just in case, so that she would be appeased again, but she walked by, annoyed, to the nurses' table to gossip about it straight-away, but I had to continue my laughter whether I wanted to or not, and if I weren't allowed to continue writing I would probably continue laughing through the night and tomorrow be sent again to the consultation room before the ungracious eyes of the most-gracious-one. Unfortunately Marianne is on night call all week, she just came in and of course also learns that I kissed Krell's, this monster's hand. How taut and severe she can hold her mouth. I bet she is thinking now: Don't worry, we will cure her of her clownish acts! . . . How fearful I am! Oh my God, why is not a single soul here with whom I could share my fear without increasing it? And Frau Lanzinger is now folding up her embroidery because she is going home and no longer needs the sojourn in the silken castle with the terrace made of cross-stitches and the cypresses of dark-green pearl yarn. Where will I find a castle and cypresses or even a dense, old, wild apple tree. Why do we keep so few of these eternal things! Once, as a child, I managed to catch a honey-brown butterfly with my always so fearful hands, and I loved it and held it for almost half a day, consoled and transfigured and suddenly believing again the existence of real angels, not merely angels in fairy tales and legends, but true ones that have a real voice, so that they can tell a timid butterfly that a little, sick girl would certainly not inflict any harm on it. Yes, that lasted for a little while, but then, when I had to hold it up to my dumb eyes – and surely superfluously – I realized it wasn't an angel at all but just a sick butterfly that couldn't fly and, for better or worse, had allowed itself to be caught. I almost would have thrown it away like something repellent, but since I was always ailing and therefore also compassionate, I placed it as gently as possible into the nearest grass. And so, dear Lord, would you place me somewhere into the grass, in disgust as well as in compassion, if I would now out of fear and illness let myself slip into your hands. You must surely want to see all of us safe and fully confident and with sole ardor approach you, but since there are no real angels to talk us intelligibly out of our fear of you, you receive us always as wounded beings and we are compelled to see you as a refuge. But I want you more and better . . . How they all

suddenly sneak around me as if I had just become visible
to them. Perhaps through the Hunchback's hand they all
touched my naked heart and now realize I am among them
as if under a united cloud. Because all who are here
belong, far beyond hate and antipathy, together spiritually.
Perhaps each one who enters here as a patient immediately
loses his own warm, poor soul in favor of a group soul?
Once, when he still considered me full of hope, Anton
talked to me quite a lot about such matters. Why should it
not be so? Plants, stones and animals have a group soul.
And are we more than animals? Or simply stunted plants
that perish. And perhaps I have long since been a part of
them, and they know more of my fear and everything else
than I want them to know. Just now the little good-natured,
gentle old woman walked by and whispered mysteriously
to me: "Here you are again. But why didn't you accept the
head of my Thomas, earlier, upstairs in the chapel? All of
my seven sons always carry their heads under their arm on
Sundays, and Thomas, my youngest, wanted to give you
his. Without a doubt he would have married you later on,
but you didn't accept him, so dumb, so dumb, my
handsome Thomas with his blond locks on his head, no,
you shouldn't have done it, not that. But they are coming
again. Tonight all seven are coming upstairs into the
chapel, and then you have to be clever. I'll give you my
blessing in a flower pot, and if you tend it carefully, it can
even survive the winter here. For all the other daughters-
in-law I poured poison into their gruel because they all

have such false, receding, contorted eyes and hearts made
of mica, I can't stand that, it glitters so much in the sun,
but you don't need to be afraid because of that, I'm just
going to cut off your head so that you match each other
even better. You are definitely going to come, aren't you?
Into the chapel, don't forget, will you?" . . . I promised her
everything, and now she is standing there under the loudspeaker and pretending to practice a dance. I wonder what
chapel she has in mind? We are never allowed to enter the
institution's chapel because we are dangerous, after all,
and could attack the others. I wonder if she really has
seven sons? But now, after the episode in the bath, I
probably can't make any more demands because gradually
they are convinced that my mind is not well. Nurse Marianne casts curious glances at me from time to time. I am
afraid . . . She was just here. Acted as if she was just casually passing by and wanted to look over my shoulder at my
writing. But I placed the blotting paper over it and suddenly – God knows why – I sang softly and as cheerfully as
possible: "Gather the rosebuds while you may . . ." It must
have been the nearest nonsense that occurred to me in my
state of fear. In any case it served its purpose, she recoiled
from me and probably now considers me the most crazed
of them all . . . It is good to be crazy among the crazed, and
it was a sin, an intellectual arrogance, to act as if I weren't.
Why shouldn't I too for once be wholly and completely at
home? . . . They, the ones here, are willing to accept me,
I realize now after the preceding episode. Dear, small,

delicate girl, Renate, maybe we will be friends now after all, gentle and sad as you are. I will smooth your thick, dark hair, will arrange the dreadful institutional blouse more attractively around your narrow waist and will walk up and down with you in this corridor of terror as if we were in the gardens of one thousand and one nights. I want to recite poems to you until your darkened mind gently begins to heed them, until your blood, perhaps over-burdened, flows more readily in a lovely rhythm and you truly become a Renate, reborn from the spirit. I want to love you, as every girl has to be loved at one time, to know that she was. They all moved away from you, maybe on the outside they might have been ready to love, but it must still happen here because we are here to experience life together . . . O my God! . . . My God! . . . My God!! . . .

Since I ended yesterday with this somewhat exag-gerated exclamation, I may have anticipated today's only possible beginning . . . Did I do that? Calm down, my little soul. Well, yes, why should I not call myself "my little soul"? Absolute poverty distinguishes itself primarily by being able to make do with the least amount. Ever since my mother abandoned all affection toward me because of my immensely bashful rejection, which sometimes deteriorated into hatred, – oh, how it suited her, how well she did it, as if continually prompted by angels! – but it didn't work, it did not touch me, it was like a squandering of delicacies on something totally unworthy, it always seemed to me, and then she gradually gave up, and since then it has occurred to no one to choose me as an object of affection. And yet we want to be that object again, we all want that, whether we qualify outwardly or not. An inner qualification is inherent in all of us, also in those of us who are repulsive, yes, that's how it is, my heart. To introduce a few little peculiarities here might be worthwhile in the end, but not until the end, and one probably has to begin quite generally at the beginning, in order to have steps for gradual progress. Above all, no haste, just gentleness, and it may be possible one day to discover oneself as one discovers a beloved, to coddle oneself, one will require nothing but the gentle touch of hands on the forehead or the hair, hands acting like strangers. Poverty is an excellent instructor in all subjects, why not also in love. And I want to study it thoroughly. No angel later on is expected to teach me because The-Later-On and the angels are uncertain. Uncertain is also the towering spire of these angels, the monstrous, which we try to call God, and it is senseless to contact him at a beginning, as if one wanted to tread on a mountain from above. And so I say: "my little soul, my heart!" and I say it to myself and thus I am poor yet also safe. For everything here is uncertain. Everything changes from one moment to the next, every reference is two-sided and continually crosses from the real to the unreal. Last night afforded much in this regard. I had been so roused by the very hot bath, by the grotesque outburst of the Hunchback, the whisperings of the old woman with her seven real or unreal sons that I surely had reached the outermost limit where reason and imagination meet like water and fire. And then the need, this accursed imagined need, that one is absolutely compelled to turn to another person! It was Renate I wanted to love. As if one could want a love. Yes, even if this were indeed given to us, if this were included in our free will, how differently all references to human life would turn out. I don't believe a man or a woman would then summon the severity to leave a love unrequited, why would they? Everyone prefers to give than to receive. But this way . . . I was crazy enough yesterday to convince myself of being able to give something I don't have. After dinner, a revolting mishmash of vegetables and slabs of meat which we had to fish out with our fingers as always, since only paying patients receive knives and forks – a curious practice, considering that paying patients too could injure or kill themselves with a knife, right – well, later on I went to Renate and asked her: "Fräulein, would you like to take a walk with me?" . . . You see, she likes to walk back and forth for hours, as if she had a motor in her which only the sternest nurses' command could turn off. After dinner no one is required to work anymore, and so no such command can be expected. Moreover, Nurse Marianne had gathered a small and almost intimate circle around her and seemed to want to let the others be as undisturbed as possible. Let us not forget it was a Saturday. All Saturdays have – God knows why? – something implicitly festive about them. One thinks of swept courtyards, gently swaying, clean windows in which a sunset or even a rising star is mirrored, gently curved meadow paths with puddles here and there that give way to bare feet, puddles which, like the reflecting windows, are glimmering into a deeper, inner, strange world. Everything is far more possible on Saturdays than at any other time. One always feels that something had to happen now, something that one had been waiting for continuously and for a long time, since earliest childhood. That's it, the expectation! The wonderful readiness for adventures that surely still would lie ahead. It's not life that's important, only the adventure. And perhaps they all knew that somehow, perhaps each one here still possesses a sane inner place that enables her from time to time to rest and wait. Only this solemn rest had such a strange and reverse effect here. Even the Hunchback revealed a glimmer of quiet goodness now and then in her otherwise so mean-spirited frowns, light and silky as if lit very gently from somewhere. No one raged, no one had a seizure, and whoever thinks this through, would have to admit that the age of miracles is not yet over. We just always want to see it very ostentatiously and brilliantly attired coming toward us, that's the problem. However, but this is still no proof to the contrary, the major's wife continued to scream and curse, and even though Nurse Marianne ordered the dormitory door kept shut, one heard it incessantly into the stillness outside. But she on the inside happens to have other rhythms than we, just as she had previously also experienced other ways and conditions of life. Hansi's whimpering was not noticeable because it was a part of the place like the sound of a clock. The Crucified One lay under the loudspeaker, closely pressed to the wall so as not to disturb anyone, and she also made no requests. Nurse Marianne is surely good but what's even more sure, she is not a good target for her kind of requests. And so the evening progressed, rightly or wrongly, it was a Saturday evening that demanded to be festive. The chosen circle consisted of a few teachers, a short older Fräulein who, although she was only a dressmaker, assumes a kind of special position here, but I don't mean the Ivory Princess now, who had already retired to her dormitory. The Fräulein, she is called Fräulein Hermine, is likewise an unsuccessful suicide, has a lamenting, gentle, yet somehow overbearing voice, after all her health insurance is paying for her stay here. That's significant. To Nurse Marianne's right, and suddenly like a personality, sat the singer, a mighty, full-bearded creature with occasionally eerie, wild eyes, she always snores like a motor, and when one approaches her one thinks one is in a circus, because her odor reminds one of exotic animals. But they endured it, all of them. Because she sang. She wasn't the only one, Nurse Marianne was also singing and the others were helping out according to their talent. If they had sung a folk song, a melancholy love song or just a popular hit – church hymns too for all I care –, all this would have been all right and possible in its way, but they were singing: "Early in the morning when

the roosters crow, before the quail call resounds . . ." Oh
dear God, they really did sing: "Then our dear Lord is
gently walking, walking through the woods!" . . . Just
think about it, all of you, for whom (aside from my own
poor heart) I am recording this –: here in the asylum,
behind eternally locked doors, crowded together in a
hundred varieties of madnesses, they were singing: "Our
dear Lord is gently walking, walking through the woods!"
. . . A full-bearded, semi-bestial woman who never again
will get to see any woods in her lifetime, had to sing this
song here because it was Saturday evening and a young,
pious nurse, who can go into the woods anytime she
wishes to in her free time, wanted to hear it. And I just
earlier resolved to love everyone, including her, too, and
now I felt like inflicting the greatest pain imaginable on
her. Unfortunately seizures are not at my disposal, otherwise it would have been easy for me casually to interrupt
everything; a straitjacket did not frighten me. But
dissimulation is so difficult here, much more difficult than
elsewhere, one immediately encounters all the genuine
outbursts as if they were opponents and would have to be
very practiced and strong on the inside. I am neither, and
so it was difficult. Well, well, I won't weep, . . . Buddha
may be tough and transparent like the most precious stone,
but some part of him will harbor something like mercy or
forgiveness. If everything is cause and effect, then it
contains at least, if not forgiveness, then justification. And
causes were there, they were in the Lord, walking in the

woods, who let himself be sung to in a madhouse.

But Renate and I had been walking up and down the hall for some time before this. Renate, timid and vague, always looking up to see if we have permission, then smiling soothingly at me or some other thing. It must be recorded in writing that I wanted to love her and draw her into a relationship with me. That was difficult because she lives in constant fear. But gradually I managed to find out that she loved an older shoemaker. That wasn't much and actually more sobering than shocking. And there's also a stepmother in the picture. She is the one who is opposed to it. No, Renate did not resort to any bigger words. She is simply opposed to it. She had me locked up here . . . "But," I said, "but the chief physician can't just keep you here because of that." . . . "Oh, yes, he can, he doesn't want to either. No one wants to. And then there is also the fact that if no one would be locked up here they would have to shut down the house, and they would suddenly be unemployed and wouldn't get any money to live on. The one who wanted to marry me is also unemployed even if he can construct heavenly shoes. No one wants heavenly shoes anymore, that's true, isn't it, they all think they can get up there without them, without having to spend money on them. And how is one to live then and support a family? She is right in this regard, even if she is closely related to the devil. She is his half-sister for sure, and Father should not have married her, now that we have all become kin. Then he came directly to me as an uncle and told me to hang myself, and he left me with a rope. But Father cut it off and said: You bad woman, you. And he called me a whore because she told him to, and a disgrace and a sinful brat and all sorts of other names. They will never, for the rest of my life, take me out of here. And who is to wash and mend the shirts now for the heavenly shoemaker? He has only two. But otherwise it's good that he didn't come into the devil's kinship. Don't you agree with me?" . . . "Yes," I said and would have liked to fill her sad hands with little affections, but unfortunately my awkward hands blundered, and I hid it in my heart. "I also like someone very much, Fräulein Renate." . . . "Is it also a heavenly shoemaker?" . . . After I denied this she turned her receptive face away. Probably nothing else affected her so much. But I didn't want to admit it and continued talking to her: "I have seen him only three times and never alone, but we have been writing letters to each other for years. Not many, because he has little time, he is an important man who has to help many, almost like our own chief physician." . . . "And what is your stepmother's reaction?" . . . "I don't have one. My mother says nothing because she knows nothing about it. Actually you are the only person who now knows, aside from me." . . . But this too failed to move Renate in any way, she merely turned away and asked: "Did the devil bring you a rope too?" . . . "No," I said thoughtlessly, "he merely scattered a few poems into my heart, do you want to hear them?" . . . Although she was silent, I began to recite for her as softly as possible,

yet still audibly, while walking back and forth, a few of
my silly verses. It may have gone on a bit too long for her
because when I spoke the last lines of one poem: I know
you will walk on when you see me standing at the edge of
the path, I will lay my hands into your tracks and weeping
I will think how holy you are . . . , here she raised her sad,
small face a little like one who has been annoyed, and,
fatigued, she fumbled around in her lovely hair. Of course
I blushed with shame and could not leave her like this and
yet defiantly still I wanted her to accept something from
me. Maybe I should have told her a funny little story or a
sad one or some kind of an unknown story, that would
have made her laugh or cry, something simple with step-
mothers and heavenly shoemakers, angels and devils and
such, but at that moment they were singing: "Walk softly
. . ." Many kinds of anger, despair, and shame and an
absolutely certain feeling for the complete ridiculousness
of my situation must have been the reason why I suddenly
began, loudly and quite distinctly audible to many: "Dear
Fräulein Renate, you should know the songs of Gautama
Buddha's monks and nuns. They are so artless, rhyth-
mically so wonderful and so soothing, that one should
always recite them to oneself before falling asleep. Just
listen: The rain drizzles like soft songs. The hut protected
from the wind will guard me. I have hidden my heart in my
bosom, yes, o cloud, drizzle, rain, if you wish . . . Isn't that
magnificent? . . . Or: The distant mountain tops, covered
with wild caper bushes, the roaring of elephants far away,

my craggy peak pleases me greatly . . . What do you say to this. Doesn't one become silent and light inwardly?!!" But of course she said nothing, only stared at the floor in embarrassment. The Crucified One, whom we just passed, suddenly raised her frightfully pleading hands again, and that may well have been the last cause which compelled Nurse Marianne to break out of her Saturday evening celebration. Yes, she was the one who broke out, no one else. She was very infuriated, disproportionately so. "You here, go to bed at once. What are you trying to do? I refuse to tolerate this behavior, even if you pretend to be crazy. I will see to it that the chief physician has you sent directly to bed after your daily bath. Or is the straitjacket more to your liking?" . . . I went to bed silently. Renate stood in the hallway like one who was unjustly spared, and what was hardest, although I had long since given it up, was wanting to love her. None of the others even dared to look at me.

Yet on this night I managed to sleep a little for the first time because —. No, I must not let myself be seduced to the injustice of dismissing it with a little "because–sentence." It was something bigger. I lay – eyes and face covered with my arms – for a long time, and as always I was thinking of some senseless, no, disconnected words. For example "stone." This is a method of contemplating completely and correctly the word "stone," until it becomes something heavy. And when I have reached the point where some part of me is filled with it, then comes another word, perhaps "flower." Not a specific kind of flower, that would go too far and could be distracting. But simply "flower," until something else has given up its space for it, because a flower needs space where it can thrive. And so it goes on and on. If you have spent an entire night until morning doing this, then it's possible that just when the wake-up bell shrills, you are finally at the point when your inner emptiness is gone and has become so heavy that you could fall asleep. Convinced that it would be like that again, I drifted slowly, slowly toward this increasing heaviness, when Nurse Marianne stood by my bed. I was very frightened, and that was good, because only fear prevented me from asking scornfully whether the Lord had finally walked long enough, softly, softly, through the woods. She certainly would not have put up with that without punishing me since she had come to be pleasant, and those who are pleasant are always very vulnerable and easily change into the opposite. No, I am grateful to the fear, I did not hurt her, unless it was my mere pitiful gaze that managed to convey it to a certain degree, in any case, she got over it – yes, it was good to witness that she got over something, when she addressed me with a curious smile: "Sit up!" she commanded. Yes, that's how it was, she was the first one to make use of the here so commonly used "Du" form and apply it to me. It was a stab in my heart, if I may say so, no, I can't describe this small but nonetheless definite fear-pain. I sat up, of course, we all have to be obedient here. "Here, take this!"

. . . It was water in a tin cup and an oval, rather large pill in the palm of her hand that I had to take. Since my suicide attempt had transpired with similarly shaped pills, I had thought I could never take any kind of pills at all in my life because all my nerves rebelled to the extreme at the mere thought of these medications. But her eyes were like shiny stones, and her smile was so on edge as if it could turn into a threat, so that my rebellion collapsed totally. Yes, suddenly I was as willing as an animal and not just willing, but perhaps only like a quaking animal that was no longer conscious of having hands, and simply wanted to accept everything, the water and the pill, with its mouth . . . "Good God," she said, and set the tin cup down at the edge of the commode to free a hand to bend back my head, with the other hand she let the pill all the while fall into my mouth without touching me. We looked at each other. "Please drink this, and then go to sleep." . . . My gratitude disappeared under the curses of the major's wife because her time had come again, a precisely calculated point in time had expired within her, and there she sat now, our terrible clock, held her claws vertically like fingers of a clock and screamed and screamed her inner time: "Austria be cursed, the czar of Russia be cursed –," and so on. I found it so unfortunate that this outburst had coincided with my little word of gratitude because it would have mattered so much to me to keep Nurse Marianne a little bit longer at my bedside, I felt we hadn't spent enough time yet looking at each other. But she walked on, walked from bed to bed, somehow suddenly negligently – I felt – because she spent exactly the same amount of time at everyone's bed, as if they all were equally needy, even at the empty bed of the deceased, even at Magdalena's, who lay tied up in the cell over there. But I could not reflect for very long on this fulfillment of duty, which struck me as peculiar, because all the heaviness which I slowly had to pour into me word for word, suddenly overwhelmed me, and without prior announcement, so that I was not prepared for it at all and simply resigned myself to it.

I am still completely uncertain whether that was truly "sleep." It's possible it was both the deepest sleep and yet the keenest vigil. For a long time I only had the sensation of drifting on waves, but not merely with my naked body but rather as I was, with my white-painted, chipped cot, yes, I was clearly able to read all the while the embroidered labels "National Charity Institution" on the bedspread, which was peculiarly stained with all sorts of paint. Perhaps that led more and more to the sensation of drifting toward an act of charity, and only the fear of being constantly stared at by something prevented me from completely enjoying the charity. As a very young girl I had been given for a period of time free lodgings in a convent in order to take part in a home economics class. And so one gesture of charity merged with another, so that I felt for a long time that it was a nun who was standing by my bedside, posted to supervise me. (In the beginning during my convent stay I was regarded as very depraved because of my big, sick eyes, and not until after many, almost irreparable blunders were they convinced how easily I could be guided with a little bit of kindness.) And now I was talking with this nun, swaying on the waters toward her, convinced her as well as myself that nothing more had been omitted than a little word of thanks on my part. But she wanted something else, wanted it so insistently and demandingly that there was nothing left for me to do but wake up. And then it was no longer the nun but the little kind woman with the seven sons. She was indeed standing there, tearing at the railing of my bed and constantly whispering to my feet: "I want your head, you must give me your head, they have been waiting upstairs in the chapel for so long." . . . "Go to bed," I begged her, sitting up, but she insisted on my head. It was very difficult for me to refuse her request rationally. I had to search for some time for the right words and finally managed to say: "Not today, dear woman, Nurse Marianne is watching too closely today, she wouldn't allow it, but maybe tomorrow. We'll get it done some time, but right now you better go to bed." . . . That's how well I had already mastered this sort of half-reasonable, half-crazed persuasion to make her leave me and my bed. She continued to stand for quite some time before Magdalena's empty bed, as if she were contemplating whether it contained a bride for her Thomas. The rest of the night was peaceful, and I slept through it until the ringing of the morning bell, which seemed to pulse through each of my bones. And then it turned out that Nurse Marianne had done even more for me, because she allowed me to sleep until the doctors' rounds.

I was called away to the visitors' room. Anton had returned. Are matters so visibly awful that I deserve a look like that? Usually he doesn't let his worries show so readily, this apostle of Buddha, always a bit superior to everything, and now he looks at me as if he had suddenly discovered a stone in front of him over which he needed to jump but had no desire to do so. Beta had a lot of work, he said, but of course it was her own fault because she simply failed to arrange things in such a way that time would remain for her own inner moral edification. I almost burst into laughter at the mere thought of Beta having to edify herself on top of all the other things she had to accomplish. And as if she needed to! If only all of us would be as whole and healthy inwardly as Beta, then there would be little need for any further edification. But of course I didn't share these thoughts with him, although, even as an adversary, he would have treated me gently. He asked me about the "young blonde" and meant Magdalena. Had every one of our words and gestures not been spied upon, I would gladly have given him further details about her, just to observe to what degree he is capable of maintaining his equanimity. A visible warmth as the last time did not rise up again between us, although I was very moved that he had not forgotten to smuggle a few cigarettes in for me with the new books. I'm afraid it's

because with every passing hour here I blur the relation-
ships with the outside world. I let most of his words drift
past me as if he were talking to someone else, while
inwardly I could not get rid of the curious notion of identi-
fying myself somehow with the blue lightbulb, which is
turned on at night in our dormitory room. And therefore
everything affected me so little, I merely had to be here
and cast light upon all sorts of indescribable horror. Words
had very little to do with me, even then when I heard them
and forced myself to respond to them. How will things be
after the six elapsed weeks? Will I ever be able to think
and talk again so that a kind of intelligibility can arise
between me and the others? Ah, I am so afraid, and from
hour to hour the fear changes, and each one is greater than
the previous one, although one wouldn't have considered
it even remotely possible. Sometimes I stand at one of the
barred windows and cling to it, for when the streetcar
outside passes by, one hears not just its varied noises but
there is also a peculiar trembling throughout the whole
building, and I hold on and accustom myself to regard it as
something positive, to sense the last repercussions of the
noise and the motions from outside. Yes, I can imagine
that I could attain a kind of peace here, if suddenly I were
told I had to stay here forever. Of course, at first I would
have one crying fit after the other, but after these were
overcome I would know a place from which one could no
longer be driven out. And that would be a lot. At least one
could put to use every notion of arranging oneself

permanently here, and wouldn't have to think about "later" after every virtually unattainable expenditure of effort. And this "later" would demand exactly the opposite effort which one certainly will no longer be capable of.

The "Ivory Woman" did come after all to fetch me, and we spent a rather festive hour together. Of course I lost again, but this time she must have reconciled herself beforehand to having a lesser and unteachable opponent, and so she concealed her impatience behind a gentle smile peculiar to her. We barely said a word, it also was unnecessary. At one time the eternal Rosary-sayer fell down just in front of us, looked up in confusion as if something illicit had happened. One really gets used to all sorts of painful situations very quickly, and in time it becomes understandable why the doctors are able to pay their visits with the same friendly, imperturbable smiles. What is odd and pathetic, however, is that again and again every face turns to them with such an expectant, indescribably hopeful expression as if they were saviors making an appearance. Then I observed all, the poorest as well as the very refined and reserved, they all resemble each other to such an extent as if they had suddenly received the same face. I am sure I too don't look much different, even if I can determine it only on my hands, which become restless every time, as if they were finally permitted to hold on to something. Of course one must not let that pass, and so I now always make an effort whenever the doctors' rounds take place to conceal my hands in the

71 of 114 placement

loose, striped institutional gown.

A new patient just arrived. She came over from Section "Three," from the difficult cases. The nurses call her Frau Cent and smile at her encouragingly now and then. I am afraid that won't go on for long because the woman seems to have an extraordinary urge to talk and she envelops the poor nurses with her words and gestures so persistently and extensively that these, while still trying to smile, communicate with meaningful glances.

I visited Frau Lanzinger, spent the duration of a brief half hour in her completed embroidered castle, and in passing found out that her little girl will be confirmed next year and that her friend, for whom she still harbors "maternal feelings," finally got a job as a watchman. She also asked me if I thought she should marry him in spite of the age difference; when I advised her to do so she became very cheerful and felt she could talk so agreeably and sensibly with me as with no one else. Yes, she seemed to feel so very much alone with me in her castle that she failed to notice the gently admonishing looks of the other nurses and even began to engage in happy, carefree teasing. She congratulated me on my friend and considered it understandable that one had more than mere maternal feelings for such a handsome, kind gentleman. When I looked at her rather baffled – because I failed to understand – she felt she had to console and encourage me and predicted that he would not become unfaithful to me, otherwise he wouldn't show up so regularly. Ah, dear

Lord, she was referring to Anton! It was very difficult for
me to repress my rising laughter and turn it into a hopeful
smile, but I understood at once this necessity and
simultaneously the sudden way out that offered itself to
me. I am still a little queasy when I think of the possibility
that presented itself to me: in the guise of this assumption
which, no doubt, was already spreading among all the
nurses and perhaps even among the physicians.

When Anton returns tomorrow I will be particularly
happy and affectionate. Oh, I can do it, I can surely do it!
For days to come there must be no other talk than my
unhappy love for Anton, my brother-in-law. And then –
and then – . . . But now it is becoming so difficult to wait
for the days to come. I no longer understand how I was
able to endure the weeks – yes, it has been two solid weeks
–. Winds, clouds, and birds were supposed to help me, but
they didn't do anything, oh my Lord, no, I would have felt
it if they had done even the slightest thing. I am certain he
has long since forgotten how it was before I came here.
Ah, he had already forgotten me by then, long since, and
then he was startled and merely looked at me and was
startled . . . "You? . . . You . . . Fräulein, well, yes, please
do come." . . . And all the while he looked up at his wife
– she must have been his wife, because he smiled at her
and called her to witness his poor memory for faces –:
"Fräulein is wearing a different dress – and you know how
I am when even you happen to walk by me on the street
with a new hat on, I think every time: shouldn't I know

this woman? . . ." And they were so united in their kind, warm laughter they didn't realize how horrified and rejected I was standing there. And even then after his wife had left the consulting room – still smiling – I continued to stand there looking at him, just at him, and felt that things would finally turn out differently, and I would still be spared the asylum. He asked how I felt, and when I replied that I had decided after all, as he once suggested, to enter an asylum to calm my nerves, he exclaimed almost joyfully: "Bravo! That's a wise decision, now you will see that everything is doable as long as you want to do it." . . . "Yes," I said simply and wanted to scream, scream, so that he would finally understand what was being done to me with this terrible love. But he didn't even understand this one thing, that my only consolation would consist of breathing and living with him in the same city, in the same apartment complex. Oh, he placed his big, dear hands on my shoulders, and I stood before him like a small child and stared up at his white hair for so long that I grew tired and had to stop at his wonderful, kind mouth, and I must have been heavy like a burden for him so that he bent down lower than he intended, and then on my forehead I felt the soft, warm and terribly paternal touch of his lips. Ah, here I am writing it down, writing it artificially and stilted: alien, alien, alien!! And yet it was my forehead and his mouth, and now I am carrying this forehead among madmen, as if nothing had ever touched it. And no one notices anything . . . But I am forgetting the woman, that old, old woman sitting in the waiting room when he accompanied me outside. While I was putting on my coat, she raised herself on her two crutches, shuffled over to me and began a low, gentle old wives' talk as if she had prepared for it for quite some time, as if she had been waiting for me all these years to tell it. She spoke of "Herr Primarius," the chief physician, his fame far and wide, and how she had known him as a very little boy. He was so little then, she had often taken him into her lap, and now they even want him over there in America, that's how powerful and famous he is. But he's not going to leave us, we all need him, no he's not going to do that. No, Fräulein, you don't need to be so afraid, he is staying here with us ... Ah, I would have liked to listen to her until the end of my days, but when I heard his steps approaching another patient, I ran away from the old woman, impolitely without greeting and gratitude. On the stairs I almost tripped over a stranger, I was so deaf and blinded by tears. Then I came here. And here I have been holding out, for almost three weeks! No, birds, wind and clouds do nothing for me, these may well serve other lovers, such who find it easier to touch the beloved's heart. Nothing touches him, I feel it, he has long since forgotten that I am here and my forehead is here, which he has touched and driven mad. But he is not to get off so easily, no, not so easily! He must see me in my present state, in the striped institutional uniform reaching down to my ankles. It must come to light to what extent lovers live in safety and untouchability, how large are the vestibules of their hearts, in which the drama of those seeking admission takes place, again and again and again . . . Neither he nor to an even greater degree I must be spared this confrontation, which is to gain a validity far beyond both of us . . . Ah dear Lord, am I adopting the wrong means? Is it really necessary to deceive one's own soul to such an extent? I want to see him, to see him at any cost. To know once more how it feels to stand small and impoverished before him, to have the opportunity once more to hear his voice, to absorb it forever in one's hearing. Then, after I have experienced it one more time, I can go home perhaps into my village, like a dove I can pass by the houses where children will be standing, many children who already know where I am coming from and they will shout it out to each other that this is the "madwoman," she, for whom their fathers have to pay such high taxes, and the grownups will tell them to be quiet because madmen are dangerous after all. All this will then be possible, also the nights at home in my childhood bed that is so short that I'd have to stretch out my legs between the railing. Mother and my sisters will be bearable, always with their certain inner voice, and some kind of work will be offered, washing clothes or knitting stockings, everything will be possible then . . . But how much longer —.

It is evening, and I have bathed again. This time even the rounds were made while I was lying in the water, eyes and ears shut, always thinking of one voice, of only one

voice. Frau Lanzinger, who was sitting by me and did me
the favor of letting as few as possible of the others inside,
then told me that the Great Doctors had stood in front of
me for a long time and one had said: "What's the matter,
this is a well-built and handsome woman." . . . Ah, Lanzinger, she is so clumsily kind. But she will be useful, I
have convinced her that I love my brother-in-law only
platonically, that I have already gotten over my suffering
for him, and I was certain that after the course of six
weeks I could leave this place completely cured. She was
greatly affected by my nobility of soul – as she called it –
and invited me to come and visit her after my discharge in
her home, where she might also be able to introduce her
friend to me. I know it is disgraceful to deal like this with
a good-hearted person, but she won't be diminished by it,
only I. And as far as I am concerned there is nothing left to
ruin, ever since I have decided to resort to this means for
my formerly so noble love. Since then I consist of nothing
but shame, but I cannot abandon the plan. If there were
enough angels they would have to arise now to prevent it,
but even if they succeeded I would fall into their arms and
say: Let me, let me! . . . For none was present at the time
when I, poorest of the poor, stood before him for the first
time and discovered that people can also be like that, so
generous and pure into the last movement of their hands
and the most fleeting gaze of their eyes.

No, what was not prevented then must not ever be
halted now, at least that's how I understand the mission of

this so unfathomable and hopeless love.

Frau Cent deprived me of the afternoon. It was precisely as I had feared. The nurses had quickly grown
weary of her and wanted to be alone together and talk
sensibly about their own concerns, and so they simply let
her loose on me. She had been told I was a very educated
Fräulein, and one could speak to me about everything. Ah
dear Lord – and that's what she then proceeded to do at
length. She is the wife of a senior teacher and has a
daughter, who would soon make a good match, only she
herself would have to regain all her health first. She had
been brought here much too hastily, she felt, she was only
a bit too overwrought from the many séances she had
previously taken part in. No, she did not forgive the
physicians at all for not realizing at once how wrongly she
was confined here. And moreover she had been placed
among the very troubled patients and held for days in the
straitjacket simply for listening to an inner voice and
wanting to write and write. "You are writing too, and no
one is preventing you," she said almost accusingly, "but I
was supposed to resist my voice, but it was so powerful
within me that I was still writing with the straitjacket on
and with my bare toes. But no one wanted to believe me,
can you imagine, no one. Yet they are educated, these
Great Doctors, and claim to be cultured." I found this
outburst very embarrassing, and so in order to distract her
I asked what the voice had commanded her to write. With
this question I did her the biggest favor because she could

follow her imagination endlessly. It affected me oddly now to hear that a follower of Buddha was the one who spoke to her. Of the transmigration of souls, of the eightfold path to enlightenment – I believe that's what she called it – of the ascent of Brahma in the prepared and purified soul, ah, it was all so confusing and barely within my own sudden realization that I was listening to her less willingly and deliberately than she would have required. But still, she remained so grateful and devoted, called me the only understanding soul here and did not shy away from maintaining it was karma that had led us together here, in order to be purified and consoled together. Many sublime minds, like Goethe and Schopenhauer, had already materialized with her assistance, and now she was being compelled to live here among madmen, and not even her relatives had sufficient understanding for her, otherwise they could not have brought her here. But perhaps it was necessary, she felt, to guide my still swaying soul toward the truth of the sublime. "I love you," she said later on and almost would have embraced me, all the nurses laughed except for Frau Lanzinger who looked at me encouragingly and, filled with awe, thought of my platonic love. It almost turned into an unpleasant afternoon, but it taught me to deal cautiously with the books Anton was bringing me, among which there were always some containing Buddhist teachings. One is so much exposed to such dangers, and I am amazed that the chief physician had no objections when he once discovered me reading such a book. Frau Cent, thank God, has been assigned to a different dormitory, I think she would be even more difficult to endure at night. Nurse Marianne just entered, I will have to go to bed quickly. I hope she will learn as soon as today of my love for Anton, my brother-in-law. That would ease much between us. Yes, they are talking about me already, I'm noticing it, thank God! Everything will now become wonderfully lucid and that is such a relief.

I managed to sleep without a pill last night. It was no longer necessary to think of flowers or stones, everything was to lead to the coming encounter. There was much to consider, how to convince the chief physician without arousing even the slightest suspicion, and then the going to the other section? Who might be assigned to accompany me? I hope it won't be Friedel, she has such alert eyes. And then the other thing, the terrible thing, —. Will he not only understand it but also forgive me for not sparing him? . . . I fell asleep with the notion that he could weep over what is happening to both of us. Ah, why not? Why shouldn't he too be able to weep just once, since I have spent so many nights weeping and gathering grief that there could be enough for both of us. His smile is so strange and he distributes it among so many so that almost nothing substantial is left over for individuals, but if we both would experience a common grief at least, that would be much, and one surely would benefit from that for some time. But I have to go to bed before Nurse Marianne forces me to do so.

I no longer have much free time, yes, I virtually have to steal my hours for writing because Frau Cent besieges me like a fortress. The nurses are fiendishly pleased, yes, I assume they are ascribing qualities to me as obscure and exaggerated as their imagination allowed. Because she wants to be redeemed by me, something she tries to convince me of again and again, spitting with excitement. Then I usually sit there with exhaustion and can barely utter more than "yes, yes." A No or some other kind of rejection is out of the question for this agitated, fanatic will. She pursues me so steadfastly with her ardent and almost bitter adoration that I forget virtually all other fears over the concern of escaping from her. But it is completely futile to hide here, there are no nooks, no door can be locked, not even those of the toilets. Wherever I go she sneaks after me with her mysterious face, wants to receive truths of salvation from me or present her own mysterious voices. It affects me all the more deeply since I have lost virtually all sympathies overnight – ever since I have been cast into my own expectation. It is shameful, yes, but my love cares little about how it is overwhelming me. How sweet and bitter it made my night yesterday! . . . God Almighty, if this miserable woman shows up one more time, I will scream at her, I will curse her in the name of Buddha and all founders of religions, she robs me of the last bit of reason. She was just here and wanted to know in which heaven Anando – or whatever the name of

Buddha's favorite follower – was. "In the ninth," I replied desperately, whereupon she fell into sobbing rapture because until now she had known only of seven heavens, and now she felt blessed and infinitely enriched. "Nine heavens, oh all you saviors, nine heavens, what promises are you making me, a poor sinful woman! Nine heavens, and that for a mere follower, but where then is the Sublime One himself?" . . . Yes, and now I was also expected to make that discovery for her, I the initiated, the Sybil, as she called me and then tearfully embraced. If she returns, I — . The physicians just made their rounds, and Herr Primarius, the chief physician, was noticeably friendly and praised my good behavior so graciously – yes, yes, he had heard various things, well done, just continue to be good and sensible, right, that's why we are here – he had also suddenly learned of my positive influence on other patients and smiled benevolently on me and Frau Cent, my bodyguard, no, I didn't have the heart to complain. I am content now, and maybe tomorrow I will ask for an interview with the most gracious one. He will not deny my request, I know, and the suspicion, the dreaded suspicion, will not arise, no, because I do love Anton, my brother-in-law. Yes, I now seem comprehensible and therefore also more likeable to them. Nurse Marianne serves as the best example for this. Last night she was sitting by my bed for a long time, embroidering a linen set and talking about love in general, and how sensible and intellectually superior people could transform it into altruistic love and

love of God. Yes, yes, I said several times and through my
thin pillow I could feel my written words and thought: If
only you knew, if only you knew! . . . Very peaceably she
left me then to turn on the blue lightbulb. She asked
whether I wanted a pill, but I thanked her, saying I wanted
to remain awake and alert to contemplate future events.
Strange – now that I suddenly placed no importance at all
on sleeping, I began to dream quickly and almost
unconsciously. One time someone tore at my bed, and I
think I maintained in my dream that I no longer had a head
and Thomas would have to look for another bride, in any
case his good little wife looks at me today quite sadly and
hurt, without making any further suggestions. But my
dream, no, I must not stop describing it, although it is an
unmitigated madhouse-dream. I was — .

If I should ever smash my head against the wall it is
this woman, this Cent, who is at fault. She wanted to know
what I thought of Annie Besant, whether she was an
initiate or merely a sectarian heretic? . . . "Heretic!" I said
enraged but that did not drive her away, instead it filled
her with such enthusiasm that her gray short hair almost
crackled. "You are blessed, blessed!" she shouted again
and again so that it was even too much for the nurses and
Friedel called over: "Shut up, or you'll get it!" She became
docile at once because she was inordinately afraid of the
straitjacket, then I felt sorry for her after all, and I did not
mention the nasty things I had prepared for her, but
resorted as much as possible to a pretty shabby lie: "Frau

Cent," I said, "you mustn't bother me now for some time, please, because it's possible that a very big spirit wants to communicate with me. You know yourself how it is if you have to write, don't you, one doesn't write oneself, but someone is writing within us, God knows what kind of wisdom can come to light. But one needs quiet for that. Please remember that. No doubt it will also be good for you to retire and wait very quietly until the voices return. Don't you agree?" . . . She did indeed calm down now as if she had been given medication, she just looked at me for some time as if I were a holy statue, and now she is pacing back and forth at the lower, dark end of the corridor. My lie is not becoming any less shabby because of this, because I required it for my sake, but still, I am surprised that those who have been assigned to calm and soothe the inmates here do not make the necessary effort to empathize with the curious thought patterns of the patients in order to discover the place where they need to exert an influence. Surely it would often be much easier than one assumes, and with a few appropriate words one would succeed more than with injections and straitjackets. But maybe I am wrong in this matter, certainly because this one person alone almost drives me to despair, and the physicians have to cope with hundreds. If they wanted to empathize with every madman, how would their own self fare? To neutralize us may well be the only thing that can be demanded of people, everything else must be achieved by a higher being. Likewise it is probably no mere coincidence that most of the inmates hear voices, some also have visions, and perhaps those are the truly blessed. I wished I could also hear and see, but my blessing does not extend that far yet. Am I becoming too derisive? Have I become bitter already? The dream was terrible and grotesque. All right–; but does it give me the right to apply it to reality? Prophetic dreams are much rarer than one assumes, and most likely might not exist at all if one wouldn't summon their verification later on more or less consciously. And yet, and yet–there is so much left to prove. I admit, even if I were convinced that our encounter – which surely will be the last one – would transpire as impossibly as my dream had announced, I would not abandon it. Perhaps I have thus already crossed the border where love still is love and nothing else, and now I am merely approaching an experiment? Tomorrow in any case it must be. I am not planning to wait any longer. In my situation that is a daring assertion, but not too daring, my child, not too daring. Tomorrow it will be, I am ready to love all my brothers-in-law, and there are already four of them, madly. Tomorrow I'll go there no matter what – and I require no voice to tell me that. I shall be the voice this time, it will convince the Herr Primarius in the course of tomorrow to send me into the other section, with or without a nurse. Why else do I harbor, as has been established, every kind of illness within me. Tomorrow I shall let myself be treated once again as an outpatient. The certificate of poverty has long since been furnished, what more is needed. If only the

Ivory Woman would come! I long for her noble and opaque serenity. But she sees through me. Just as well. My child, we will survive it alone, certainly. No, it doesn't occur to me to leave anything to chance, which has taken precious little care of me all these years, as if I didn't exist. Until now – today I will set things straight – I alone had to take fate into my hands, whereas others let themselves be guided by it. I sought out love for myself, I needed it badly to make a clean break with so-called adolescence, I nourished and raised this love completely alone, and now I will gather and enjoy the fruits no matter how they turn out. To abandon something to chance, should it even have the mercy of making an appearance at last, would be misplaced magnanimity. I have been living for weeks now among madmen and thus have the right to resort to their oddities. If he let it come to this, to let me walk around, behind bars, in the gray, striped institutional gown, then I also have the right to act correspondingly. What? – Would that border on hate? Has everything changed completely overnight? Renate, Renate!! . . . There she is mending stockings and continuing to love her heavenly shoemaker. Why has nothing changed in her? But he returned her love, or at least she lives in that delusion. Dear, dear Lord – if you exist, if you really still do exist somewhere, then please send me this delusion too, send it to me tonight, during this last night, before the dream comes true – because I will make it come true, as surely as I am living here among nothing but madmen.

I was crying again so much that Nurse Minna had to put me to bed. Then Anton came. It was announced to me like a message of salvation, and it took some effort on my part to appear appropriately delighted. Anton is a good person. He brought me a small, red apple. "Go on and eat it, you have grown even thinner," he said and was truly concerned. He is usually not so easily concerned, not he, but I am so fond of him now as I never before would have thought possible. Peter, my other sister's husband, has never been here, Anton thinks he might have found some temporary job. That would be good, because Mara is not as clever as Beta, and they also have a little child. How long has it been since I have seen a child? It seems much longer to me than it could actually have been. Arno has such a sweet, sleepy little face, like a young Japanese, and while playing he supposedly tends to mumble to himself: "Rudolf Teiner says this and Rudolf Teiner says that. Mommy, it's Buddha, isn't it, not butter?" . . . To Mara's great annoyance, Peter always brings anthroposophists and Buddhists to the apartment, and then there is talk of nothing but such things. But she does not let herself be dissuaded from going to church, and that often leads to very bitter fights. And all this began with what we call love. Strange. One would think the entire world consisted only of fragments of love and was wonderful. But by God, that's not the case! Somehow we always bungle the fragment we are to add to the large mosaic –. And tomorrow I will go to bungle mine. Today I still want to pray.

Three days have passed, and now I am continuing.

Take care! Nothing must be added and nothing removed, stone must be set upon stone, and when it is finished I will devote myself to the spirit. Yes, the spirit. It no longer has to concern itself much with me, for during these last three days I barely managed to escape the straitjacket. I did not rage, why should I?, but they did think I would simply vanish from under their hands if they did not take action against my weeping with all the threats at their disposal. Herr Primarius has always protected me from that. "Patience, patience!" he said to the nurses, "just have patience, it will pass, and no one can weep forever."

I'm afraid – oh no, I'm no longer afraid of anything –, I just assume that he partly senses the connection and is so considerate for that reason.

This is what happened –: My dream literally came true. No, I am not laughing. Why would I laugh. If I had children one day I would tell them: "Children, don't laugh, laughter was invented by the devil." – and that might be the only truth I would have to give them. For I returned to the asylum laughing. Of course Nurse Friedel accompanied me, and since she thought I was so likeable and funny on the walk back, I also managed to find out about a romance of hers, one of them, I don't recall which one, in any case maternal feelings did not play a part in it. Now she is very upset with me because my three-day-weeping has proven her confidence in me as unwarranted. Now they all have come to consider me as really crazy too, and they no longer understand why Herr Primarius still allows me to write. I too am afraid he will forbid it one day – perhaps tomorrow already, and so I am in a hurry. All right then: Nurse Friedel led me to the other institution where I was to be treated as an out-patient. I had obtained Herr Primarius' permission so suspiciously easily that I should have been worried. But I harbored quite different worries. Then we arrived. As always I immediately felt the peculiar solemnity which must have its origin in the absolute adoration and veneration that one shows for the powerful man there. And then his voice. It resounded as if prearranged, immediately, as we entered the white waiting room, and as always it weakened me deeply into my heart. I was so pale that Friedel even asked me if I was unwell. But there was no time left, he appeared, and she had to introduce me and explain my ailment. I convinced myself that he too had grown a shade paler, in any case he did not say a word, but guided me into the little cabinet where individual consultations took place. "Yes?" he then said, nothing else. We couldn't stand around like that forever, we both knew that. But he found nothing. I gave him a long time to find something. Had he raised his hands or merely lowered his eyes. No, he did nothing, and so I now had to do my part, as the dream had prompted me to do . . . "Kiss me! . . . You have to kiss me." . . . "Child –." But it came too late. "Please!" I said, more bluntly than in the dream. "But I have a head cold," he replied. I was aware of that but it did not help him. Then he walked toward the door and I almost felt relieved that the dream had come true only to this dreadful beginning, but he merely called for his blond assistant and asked: "Fräulein, please bring me the mask." "Yesss, Herr Primarius," she sang with her high, rather affected voice. I was familiar with that too. No, there was nothing new in any of this. Angels should have intervened at this point, but they did not appear. The blonde brought the mask, withdrew discreetly, and we were still standing there. But now he looked like someone who would go to war with a gas mask. At any rate, he seemed to have sufficient courage since he took it upon himself to remain alone with an obviously mad woman. Then he kissed me. On the forehead, like the last time, and thus he erased the beautiful "last time." Now I won't have to be on my guard anymore when I bathe. I was also not spared his gentle: "Well." No, I was spared nothing. Then I began to laugh inwardly, softly. He stepped aside, stepped outside and sent in the blonde. "Child," she also said, and I would have liked to hate her for it, but it wasn't possible, suddenly we came very close to each other and she held me and we wept. That had not gone according to my dream, or maybe I had been startled out of my bed a bit too early, in any case I had no answer for our soft, mutual weeping. Thank God we had only a little time left, his slightly altered voice called from outside, and we both obeyed it instantly. Nurse Friedel received me again like a piece of merchandise, and it wasn't until our walk back, when I became so carefree, that she thought I was a person with whom she could talk quite sensibly. Perhaps we even took some detours on account of her romantic story, at any rate decades seemed to have passed since we had left the asylum. In a window pane, however, I determined that I hadn't changed noticeably, simply that I was suddenly able to laugh so beautifully. But then, the devil – or whatever name we like to give him – always does his work, – our loudspeaker inside played: "And I kissed her only on her shoulder . . ." . . . "That's wrong," I said to someone, "that's not how it goes, it goes like this: and I kissed her only on her forehead, and yet she still got my cold'." . . . "Delightful!" someone said, but by this time I was crying already and fell over a table and did not stop crying and falling until they carried me off to bed.

So that's how it was, and an expert can not detect the new gradation in the mosaic. I say we are surrounded by devils who like nothing so much as disguising themselves as love, and we can participate quite happily when we pretend to love. In truth we are more capable of doing everything but summoning up even a grain of genuine love. Supposedly God loves us. . . But he merely toys, no, not even that, he simply arranges, it gives him pleasure to look on when we use our heart, enthusiastically, piece by piece, to dress up in a radiance that glitters like love and casts lights in all possible variants. We don't love, we dance like moths around the artificial light. But – it just occurs to me, how did this nocturnal animal excite and then finally kill itself when there was no artificial light yet? Ah, who will tell me that? Was there ever so much natural light present that the nights too were enriched by it and the frenzied ones could be satiated without becoming fatally injured? . . . Was there ever such a thing? . . . Here are the dead. Here I am too and want to stay here forever. I know it is no longer difficult to convince those who matter that I belong here for the rest of my life. It will be my task to mend blue institutional stockings and simultaneously hear voices whispering this and that to me. I am still deaf but surely one can train one's hearing with some effort, just a fraction of the effort one has exhausted up to now to convince oneself of love. Surely God has nothing against losing a player since enough frenzied souls are still at his disposal who can do it better and more naturally. I was not able to, and now I have to catch up learning everything in a new subject matter. My subject matter will be the art of going crazy, and with time I shall become an expert, a Frau Primarius, isn't that so.

Frau Cent pussyfoots around me piously, and it's only a matter of making up a few more heavens to go along with the other nine, then I will stand here and will be worshiped like —, like — . . . No, I love him, I still love him, everything I said against it is untrue, his shoulders were so stooped when he left me, and his eyes did not bear it . . . But what I did to him only a madwoman could do, and so I must become mad. Tomorrow perhaps I will already be in Section "Three" and wearing the straitjacket and where I can at most write with my toes, and therefore today I am writing it once more and once again: "I love him, I love him!" . . .

Tomorrow the six weeks are over, and I am supposed to leave.

They cured me here. Yes, I must assume I am cured because they are not keeping me on, although the court psychiatrist had approved at least one year for me.

Afterword
By Ursula Schneider and Annette Steinsiek

1

The *Memoirs from a Madhouse* had been slumbering since the death of the translator and writer Nora Wydenbruck (1959) in one of numerous sealed boxes in her extensive literary estate in London.

This literary estate was not organized and assessed until the mid-1990s. When we became aware of the monograph, we took a special interest in the contact that took place between Nora Wydenbruck and Christine Lavant. We learned about Nora Wydenbruck's history of the translation of *Aufzeichnungen aus einem Irrenhaus* [*Memoirs from a Madhouse*] and also found a copy of their correspondence. From Christine Lavant's letters we were acquainted with the title *Aufzeichnungen aus einem Irrenhaus*. However, we were searching for the text: it had never been printed and was found neither in Christine Lavant's estate nor in other collections. Now we became acquainted with its English translation. But where was the German original? In the extensive catalogue of Nora Wydenbruck's literary estate we came upon the following entry under the Christine-Lavant-papers: "MSS German without a title page (it begins with: "I am in Section 'Two.' That's the observation ward for the 'slighter cases,' and one has a right to it only if one has done Section 'Three' already . . ."). A trip to London established certainty: the complete German typescript of *Aufzeichnungen aus einem Irrenhaus*, identified and compared to the English translation, was intact.

2

The translator and writer Nora Wydenbruck, born in London in 1894, raised in Carinthia and Vienna, finally settled in 1926 in England, had traveled to the continent in January 1951. Through an editor she made the acquaintance of Christine Lavant on March 14, 1951, in Klagenfurt. A correspondence ensued; Nora Wydenbruck began to translate prose by Christine Lavant in order to introduce her in England; the translations evidently were finished in late 1951. In spite of her efforts to find a publisher, neither this book nor any of the texts ever appeared in print. Christine Lavant was introduced to the English public only once (if one disregards Nora Wydenbruck's lectures and articles about "Modern Austrian Literature,") with Wydenbruck's unpublished translation of *Aufzeichnungen aus einem Irrenhaus*. From her translation Nora Wydenbruck had produced a radio play, which the BBC broadcast on November 10, 1959, read by the actress Joan Plowright. Nora Wydenbruck, who died in August of 1959, did not get to hear the broadcast. The BBC does not have a copy of the tape.

3

We first hear of *Aufzeichnungen* on December 16, 1950. Christine Lavant writes to her colleague Christine Busta: "I am beginning to worry now and to reproach myself for not having sent you the *Aufzeichnungen* by registered mail. Did you receive them?" On December 20 she follows up: "Did you get my *Aufzeichnungen*? If not, let's just forget about it, my publisher has a duplicate." Whenever there is mention of *Aufzeichnungen* in letters or in other connections, it could be possible that it wasn't necessarily this particular text that was meant. It could even have been a different or more extensive version. It is certain that a text Christine Lavant herself entitled *Aufzeichnungen aus einem Irrenhaus* was sent to Nora Wydenbruck, that this particular text has been preserved in her literary estate, and that it is this very text. On March 21, 1951, Christine Lavant writes to Nora Wydenbruck:

> In reference to your lovely proposal: The first part of the "big" book would contain the *Krüglein*, the second the *Kind*, and the third part, I believe, is virtually ready: *Aufzeichnungen aus einem Irrenhaus*. An acquaintance in Klagenfurt has the manuscript. Of you would like to read it I could have it sent to you . . . In any case, please let me know if you would like to read this manuscript. I would immediately get in touch with my publisher and ask him about rights, but I am quite confident he will be in agreement.

Upon Nora Wydenbruck's evidently affirmative response Lavant must have asked her "acquaintance in Klagenfurt" to return the manuscript. We can safely assume it was her friend the painter Werner Berg who had it because in a letter of February 14, 1951 he wrote to her about having read *Aufzeichnungen* . . . The publisher meanwhile had asked for the manuscript to be returned; the other copy that had been sent to Christine Busta had evidently been lost. On March 17 Werner Berg responded to Christine Lavant's letter in which she seemed to have asked his opinion about the projects she and

Nora Wydenbruck were entertaining (in this letter the title
Aufzeichnungen aus einem Irrenhaus is mentioned for the first
time): "Since you specifically ask me, I do not want to hold
back my wise opinion about the 'lengthy autobiography,' the
big book according to English taste; I know very well that
everything you undertake emerges from your innermost core."
In any case Christine Lavant showed a pronounced interest in
the text and its publication.

4

Christine Lavant herself nowhere uses the concept
"autobiographical"; it also does not occur in any of her letters.
This concept was possibly raised and suggested by Nora
Wydenbruck, who may have intended it as a point of interest
for the book market.

Christine Lavant writes to Nora Wydenbruck on March 21:

My publisher was enthusiastic about it at the time, but he
absolutely demanded a "pious" ending. But I haven't quite
succeeded yet. Of course I still intend to continue with the
Aufzeichnungen, but I would require peace and time since
I am no longer as I used to be, overflowing with creative
pressure, which pressure concerns itself neither with daily
worries nor with any psychic distress. In my opinion the
book's ending should be such that the entire work could
appear under the title and meaning: *The goal of damna-
tion.* But note well, dear, kind friend, how far I still have
to walk on this path. I cannot write anything untrue and
would first have had to survive hell and somehow
approach the goal . . . But please don't think I want to
ridicule this dear, clever and truly serious pious being, oh

no, I would be happy if I could end the whole thing satisfactorily from his point of view . . . I am not strong or bad, unfortunately, only pitiful in all my concerns and exposed like a medium. And so one lives as if in purgatory, from despair to hope and back again to despair. Dear friend, please don't construe this as a lament. My laments sound different. Laments are out of the question when one expects help. This however is a realm where help from others is impossible. Everything here depends on the hidden "I." I wonder if you know, if you sense what I mean. I assume: yes!

The described "setting" corresponds to historical facts. Whatever she writes, for example, about the hospital can be verified for Klagenfurt in the 1930s: the "County Asylum" and the "County Hospital" as part of the "County Charity Institutions"; the designation "observation ward for the mentally ill"; a chief physician of the women's section of the "County Asylum." There were three classes of patients, the first two were paying patients, the third class was designed for the care of the poor, the greatest number of patients. The classes were distinguished solely by the quality of the meals and linen. The communities had to bear the cost for the destitute patients of the "asylum." "Work therapy" was also introduced for the economic benefit of the "County Charity Institutions" – there was no payment for work performed. Also the streetcar mentioned in the text directly passed by the "County Asylum."

How closely the patients of the "County Asylum" and their suffering, their behavior served as models for those persons and their illnesses in the text cannot be verified. The social climate among the patients, nurses and doctors likewise cannot

be reconstructed. There is however a reference to the figure of
Anton, made by Christine Lavant herself: On September 30,
1951, she answers Nora Wydenbruck's questions regarding the
use and standardization of names. "Let's just call Anton
(Beta's husband) Anton, since that is his real name." One of
her brothers-in-law was called Anton Kucher and devoted
himself intensively to Buddhism.

What about the central unity, the I-narrator? She writes,
she smokes cigarettes, she has many sisters, her parents are
alive, she comes from poor circumstances, she was sick a great
deal and much more – everything was "just like that." The
correspondences continue: one medical dossier confirms that
Christine Lavant made a suicide attempt with pills at age
twenty and spent October 24 to November 30, 1935, in the
Klagenfurt "County Asylum," where she was treated with
arsenic. And whenever there is a quotation from the I-
narrator's writings, we are reading Christine Lavant verbatim:
the poem the narrator recites to her fellow-patient Renate
belongs to a collection of her early lyrics, which Christine
Lavant sent to the chief physician of the Eye Clinic of the
Klagenfurt County Hospital, Dr. Adolf Purtscher, whom she
revered. (Nora Wydenbruck was married to Adolf Purtscher's
brother.) Correspondences with ascertainable reality are
numerous; there are – as far as can be proved – no changes
regarding the "I." And yet "The self is a glorious secret behind
a thousand and one miseries and never describable . . . The
truly experienced realm or rather the fragmentary mirror
images of it can be found more or less magically transformed
– poeticized in my books."

Writing makes sense to Christine Lavant only if it is a
matter of "truthfulness" not of literary coquetry. She did not
dramatize here; she can "heal" herself with her writing only if

she does not conceal herself. We would like to go so far as to say that Christine Lavant in her *Aufzeichnungen* was writing about herself, about her grappling with existence, with her own existence. It is not a matter of glancing behind the wings, or reporting about unusual experiences – she is concerned with a very specific perception of reality, of existence, of the possibility of love. Writing is her means of seeing.

5

The I-figure of the text is perceived as a writer and reveals herself as a writer. She turns directly to others: "all of you, for whom I am writing this down, aside from my own poor heart." Writing is her path: "We all follow the direction into which we have been cast."

Her medical dossier states that before her admittance to the psychiatric ward she had written a "novel that portrayed the subject matter of her life," a "novel about her life." Writing is a salient part of her life; it is also a more potent as well as more binding counterdesign to an existence as a domestic servant, which is offered to the poor.

She often comes to speak of writing as a lifesaving tool. In a letter of September 30, 1951, to Nora Wydenbruck: "Yes, I was more desperate, far far more desperate, so that I saw only one solution, either a rope or a handful of rather wild poems. I tentatively chose the latter."

In a letter to an acquaintance (on October 23, 1969) she characterizes her poetry as "need/necessity" (Not-Wendigkeit): "My poetry is one of those taboos. I am ashamed because it is self-revelation. (Also an attempt at self-healing, a need/ necessity.) I no longer possess the power of turning away, what has remained is need and shame."

Christine Lavant has discovered how explosive a publication could be. On August 11, 1951, she writes to Nora Wydenbruck about the atmosphere in her hometown of St. Stefan:

> I barely dared to go to the post office because I was afraid of running into the church crowd. Acquaintances, the country folk – all are quite furious with me. I do care about their anger, but I can't do anything about it anymore. Had I suspected that my books would ever be imported to Austria, I'm certain I never would have written them. That is the difficult part about being a poet who relies only on truthfulness: one reveals events that should best be left concealed and brings them into the open . . . If I had the means I would go away from here, although I would suffer greatly from homesickness.

This experience must have been traumatic for her. Christine Lavant had hoped that the pseudonym would guarantee her anonymity yet also permit her fame. Soon this mask became useless: her writing, which at first could be protected with the pseudonym and by being published abroad, assumed a different quality as the author became more and more well known.

There is no comparably vehement insistence on her part to prevent publication as there was in the case of *Aufzeichnungen*. Christine Lavant writes to Nora Wydenbruck on February 21, 1958:

> *Aufzeichnungen aus dem Irrenhaus* must not be published. When I left the manuscript with you my situation was completely different, and yet it always felt like a

nightmare, and now I have been very sick with high fever, probably Asiatic flu plus severe bronchitis, but the doctor thought it was consumption, and so my feverish thoughts revolved seriously around death, and then nothing seemed as problematic as the possibility that these *Aufzeichnungen* might appear in print and that I could not prevent it. Please please understand me. I have nothing in this world but my siblings and they would be embarrassed and compromised and their marriages would be destroyed. When I wrote this mss. and left it with the publisher I thought the name Lavant would always protect me, that no one would find out it was me. But now everything has been revealed to all the world. Please please understand me, dear esteemed lady, please! Return my mss., burn the translation, for Christ's sake I am begging you, and I will try to compensate you gradually for the damage. My life is nothing but one huge dread anyway and if these *Aufzeichnungen* aren't eliminated from the world I have to tremble even in the hour of my death.

One wonders if she was mainly concerned about her siblings or others as well (Adolf Purtscher was still alive) or herself?

Nora Wydenbruck responded immediately after she received this letter, on February 24, 1958:

"The original German manuscript of *Aufzeichnungen* still needs to be located – I will then mail it to you. But you should not destroy it. Make a notation in the literary estate that it should 'not be published until 30 (or 50) years later.' I repeat: it is your best prose work."

The manuscript remained, for whatever reason, with Nora Wydenbruck. We have no response from Christine Lavant to

Nora Wydenbruck's letter. We would like to observe the "statute of limitation" suggestion . . .

6

In the course of the years, as the author's fame increased, her stories became more *roman à clef*-like. She never would have wanted that reception. Not all her prose texts have been dated, and that might not ever be possible, but perhaps it was the conflict of being "able to rely only on truthfulness" that prevented her more and more from writing prose. In her poetry, however, she was able to fictionalize people and events. There are published as well as unpublished poems that refer to her experience of "having spent as a young girl six weeks in an asylum after a suicide attempt"; there are poems in which one can recognize some of the situations or find words which were used to describe figures or situations. Guided by the edition of the *Collected Works* it will be rewarding to study the relationship between prose and poetry and to pursue the theme of "insanity" in her writings. *Aufzeichnungen aus einem Irrenhaus* offers a new background to the poems that have been published so far.

7

The *Aufzeichnungen aus einem Irrenhaus* are also Christine Lavant's way of grappling with metaphysical endeavors. Early in 1935 she had written to Dr. Adolf Purtscher:

> And when I look into the faces of the women who are girls
> – old girls! – and look on this or that need to lie about the

senselessness of their lives, – and I know: that will also be me! then I have nothing but scorn for myself and my efforts to distract myself; then I turn away, nauseated, from theosophy, Buddhism, theory of evolution and the like, because it seems like a lie to me. Some hours, however, become meaningful because of certain books, and then it seems as if everything were all right: It must be like that with nature! – In tranquil hours one is embraced – by its harmony – but otherwise it is only a torment. What I am saying here is not genteel and girl-like, but at least I would like to rescue the truth from the chaos.

Her medical dossier states: "Has occupied herself of late with the 'humanities,' with astrology, magic, spiritism, read many books dealing with these; she felt better as long as she was reading." The search for a metaphysical dimension becomes evident.

Christine Lavant writes to Nora Wydenbruck about the literary works that were important to her, December 5, 1951: "When I was seventeen I happened, by chance, upon the first Hamsun book, and from then on I no longer liked anything else. Gradually the Russians (Dostoevsky) made a 'chance' appearance, Lagerlöf, and very late, not until my thirtieth year, Rilke. He changed my life."

We wonder if she thus intended to indicate to Nora Wydenbruck which books were important for her and in particular for *Aufzeichnungen*: Dostoevsky and the "Russians," the "Hamsun book," *The Last Joy*, as well as Hamsun's novel *Victoria* and the *Mysteries*. Aside from possible content references Hamsun's narrative technique seems to have inspired her.

8

The medical dossier described Christine Lavant first of all as psychically troubled and, secondly, as a writer. Both descriptions attracted attention in the Nazi era. In her community she was listed in the records: the county had paid the costs of her treatment, that is, it required "documents and confirmation" that the patient was "crazy" – the bureaucratic course of events made her, so to speak, the officially notarized crazy person of the community.

In a letter of September 30, 1951, from Christine Lavant to Nora Wydenbruck, she dates the *Aufzeichnungen*: Fall 1946. Whether she referred back to the *Aufzeichnungen* written in 1935 during the weeks of her stay in the "County Asylum" must be left open. Perhaps these *Aufzeichnungen* no longer existed because she had gotten rid of them during the Nazi era? Christine Lavant must have known about "euthanasia" during the Nazi era. In the Catholic church there were certain resistances. There were cases in which relatives announced the inexplicable disappearance of patients, there were discharged patients who had witnessed or surmised events. After the war the "Niedermoser Trial" took place in Klagenfurt from March 20 to April 4, 1946: it was named after the main defendant, Dr. Franz Niedermoser; on April 4, 1966, the first judgments were passed; the *Kärntner Volkszeitung* reported the transports in March/April; on October 24 Niedermoser's execution received great media attention.

The question arises as to what Christine Lavant did during the Nazi era, what her position was, what we know about her. There are few documents about or by Christine Lavant from the Nazi era. None of her dated works falls into this period; she seems not to have written anything.

Her sympathy ("co-suffering"), her yearning for humanity, her humility in the face of existence, her skepticism about supposedly salutary ideas, her experience of always being regarded as "unhealthy," in any case as "unproductive," the experience with psychiatry – all of these make it credible that she was never "Nazi-polluted," as she wrote in 1963 to Gertrude Rakovsky, a Jewish woman. Nothing in any of her known statements indicates an affinity. In her prose she writes about discrimination, disfranchisement, violence. From a historical perspective, however, her friendships after 1945 with people who were more of less suspect seem surprising.

In the fall of 1946 Christine Lavant writes her *Aufzeichnungen aus einem Irrenhaus*. She writes about people who – if they existed – were potential murder victims. And about people who – if they existed – were perhaps murderers or accessories to murder. Between her experiences of 1935 and fall 1946 lies the historic layer of abomination – but in the text there are no evident signs of a future which was already a past for her. The cynicism and the violence-potential of the court psychiatrist, his concept of judgment, were for her an analysis of the eternally inhuman. Could one accept today Christine Lavant's words: I adhere to personal experience – without a historical experience – so that my writing remains true?

It is conceivable that with Christine Lavant's exceedingly urgent request for the return, indeed the destruction, of the text, she wanted to avoid endangering not only the marriages of her siblings and the reputation of others, but in the meantime she had also acquired more knowledge, she understood the historical dimension which made her feel ashamed of her self-absorption, the fixation on a love story.

But finally there is no need to play a historical dimension off against a personal one in the text. The text contains such a

106

comprehensive cultural analysis that historical events would "only" be a further manifestation of an illness, which expresses itself in everything and for which there is no simple diagnosis.

All references for documents and quotations can be found in the German edition: Christine Lavant, *Aufzeichnungen aus einem Irrenhaus*, Salzburg: Otto Müller Verlag, 2001.